PROBLEMS

PROBLEMS

JADE SHARMA

TRAMP PRESS

First published by Coffee House Press 2016

(An Emily Books Original)

This edition published 2018 by Tramp Press

A CIP record for this title is available from the British Library.

10 9 8 7 6 5 4 3 2 1

Tramp Press gratefully acknowledges the financial assistance of the Arts Council.

ISBN 978-1-9997008-3-6

Thank you for supporting independent publishing.

Set in 11.5 pt on 17 pt Devanagari by Marsha Swan.

PROBLEMS

Somewhere along the way there stopped being new days. Time progressed for sure: The rain tapered off through the night; near dawn, cars rumbled and then zoomed away. Sounds folded back into the world, moving on, light-years from the living room where I lay around, hardly living.

The soundtrack of the night looped every twelve hours: the hum of the refrigerator, the blare of a siren going by, the sound of someone turning on a faucet somewhere in the building. The Saturday night remix of the chatter of drunk guys, who smoked cigarettes in the courtyard and called each other 'bro,' interspersed with the chorus of drunk girls' high-pitched squeals every time a rat scurried out of the bushes.

Sometimes in the early morning, a man somewhere in the building would yell about the music being too loud. But I never heard any music. I only heard him yelling.

A buried alarm clock went off somewhere else in the building.

I puttered around my apartment in my fuzzy pink slippers, wearing purple boy shorts and a wifebeater. My husband, Peter, slept in the bedroom.

Peter. To the outside world he was my nice, handsome husband who had to deal with me. When I cried, he held me and told me he loved me. Sometimes when I cried, he said, 'Do you want some ice cream? I'll get you some ice cream.' Sometimes when I cried, he said, 'Have you run out of drugs?'

Sometimes in bed he held me as if he was a selfish little boy saying, 'Mine, mine, mine,' to the world. Sometimes he took care of me because he took care of things that belonged to him.

I was the one who lost things. I was the one who wanted to talk when it was time for bed. I was the mess, and he was the one who rolled his eyes. I was the one who bought dope with the tips he brought home. He was the one who came home drunk. Who the fuck was I to tell him he had had too much to drink when he had to deal with me? When he wasn't being a saint, he was telling me what a saint he was to put up with me.

He was an idiot. A beautiful idiot that slept at night, woke up early, went for a run, went to work, came home drunk, passed out, and then did it all over again.

Whenever a man told me he loved me, I imagined how one day this same man would tell me that I was a crazy bitch, because I am a crazy bitch.

An unlit cigarette between my lips, I looked for a light. On the coffee table: half a bottle of ginger ale, scratched-off lotto tickets, loose change, and a matchbook I kept forgetting was empty. I tried Peter's Zippo. Spark. Nothing. Spark. Nothing. Dead. I tossed it on the couch and went to the kitchen to light the cigarette off the stove. I felt like one of those women on *Intervention*, smoking alone at some weird hour.

On the couch, I pressed my fingers along my rib cage, ran my hand down my belly to the crooks of my hips. I imagined my hand was Ogden's. I stuck my hand in my underwear. I thought of how he would feel how smooth my pussy was. How his fingers would feel through the folds to my clit. How he would feel how wet he made me.

Ogden had been my professor when I was doing course work for my master's degree in English. I had always wanted to fuck a professor, like it was the kind of fuck you could check off a list: celebrity, artist, European, fireman, another girl (check), three-some (check), etc.

I got wet when I listened to Ogden lecture. I loved his deep masculine voice when he said feminine words like 'beautiful' and 'sonnet.' I watched the way he patted his chalky hand on his jeans and left a white smear like he didn't give a fuck. I thought of his deep voice in my ear, saying, 'Yeah, you like that?' The way the cuff of his shirt was unbuttoned. I saw the dullness of his eyes, as if he had spent a lifetime staring at the colour grey. I wanted to see how different his eyes would look when I looked up while I blew him.

After the semester ended, we met for a cup of coffee and ordered drinks instead. I waited for him to come on to me, but he didn't. He told stories that had the air of being told before. He ate bread like a caveman: gnawing at it, crumbs falling onto the wooden table. Why couldn't he talk to me like a normal person? Ask me about my childhood, where I was from, about Peter, and then tell me about his high school girl-friend. Volley the ball around instead of talking at me. Even when you are ready to put out for a guy, he has to go and fuck it up. I didn't care about hooking up with him anymore. I wanted to go home.

It was his idea to share a cab. I climbed into the back, my hands on the leather seat. He told the cab driver where to go. I stared at him staring out the window. He was totally content with the prospect of sitting in silence for rest of the ride and then never seeing me again. There was something about a man not caring if he ever saw me again that made me want to suck his cock.

'So you don't want to have sex with me?' I said, like it was a dare.

'It doesn't seem like it's going to happen, so maybe that's for the best,' he said.

'Yeah,' I said as I stared out the window. The way you could see all down the street between blocks. 'But you know,' I said, 'there is the conquest factor. This has been my objective for a semester ...'

He laughed. Then he said, 'Come here.'

I got on top of him, and he shoved his tongue into my mouth. *I am totally making out with Ogden Fitch*, I thought as I made out with Ogden Fitch. He didn't kiss how I imagined he would. His tongue greedily pushed into my mouth. The car pulled over to the side of the street in front of my building.

'I shaved my pussy for you,' I said into his ear.

'Aw, how sweet,' he said, looking genuinely flattered. I shoved my tongue back into his mouth.

I had been married to Peter for seven months.

It wasn't because I didn't love my husband that I had cheated on him.

Sometimes I didn't know if I loved my husband.

I didn't know. It was a marriage. Marriage is boring, and sometimes you want to kill the person, and sometimes you feel the truth of a million clichés about having one real partner to grow old with when the world is cold and full of strangers. But most of the time I didn't feel anything.

Seeing the same person so much makes you not see them at all. Sometimes I awoke from the haze of the living-room-watching-television funk and that fuzzy figure next to me on the couch would come into focus: a real-life human being whose mind was as vivid and whole as mine. I would think to myself,

Who in the fuck is this person? And I would ask, 'Peter, what are you thinking?' And he would say, 'Nothing, really.'

Lorrie Moore wrote, 'For love to last, you had to have illusions or have no illusions at all.'

Sometimes I tried to hold on to him, but I was always losing my grip, and he was always fading into the background.

I had cheated on every man I had ever been with. It was stupid to think there was something wrong with loving more than one person at a time. Sometimes the thought of who put their thing in whose thing seemed like the most absurd thing in the world to be concerned with. I thought I might as well as fuck as many people as I could before my cunt dried up and nobody wanted me anyways.

You shouldn't put out right away. That's what I'd heard. I had no idea because I'd never not put out right away.

After I started having an affair, Peter and I fought less. Sometimes I thought we were closer than we'd ever been.

I never imagined any man would ask to marry me. I wanted to try it on: a grown-up's life of grocery lists, laundry, and arguments about who was supposed to buy new light bulbs. Peter was a badge I wore that said to the outside world, 'How crazy can I be if this normal person has decided to spend the rest of his life with me?'

I didn't know what to do when men gave me flowers. I would always think, *Great, now I will have to watch these things die.*

Sometimes I tried on this fake woman persona, and I knew Peter liked it because he got to try on his version of a male persona. I put my hair up and talked in a high-pitched voice and moved my hands around, all animated, like Elizabeth. I talked about how I wanted to get my nails done. Sometimes I would put lotion on my hands. I acted stupid so he could feel smart.

Sometimes I was in love with who I was with when I was with him.

If I didn't try to act feminine, I felt like a dude.

A few more lines. You shouldn't do too much because then you will have to do more to get the same effect, but then again this was the last of it, so you may as well get blasted.

Nothing was on television.

Raymour & Flanigan. I could hear the catchy jingle just seeing those words on the TV. Then some middle-aged man looking out a window. A commercial for DeVry University. Can you imagine your life being so shitty you'd call up DeVry University to get a degree in computer animation?

Drip down the throat. Warmth spreading out, like pee on a blanket. Music from the speaker plugged into the laptop.

'And the sun pours down like honey / On our lady of the harbor, / And she shows you where to look / Among the garbage and the flowers …'

Dope felt like leaning back in a chair, and right before the chair tipped over, it froze, and there I was, suspended in midair but not falling at all.

I heard Peter's alarm go off. Eight o'clock. I snorted what was left on the book.

The door wasn't easy. You had to jerk it.

'How you feeling?' Peter asked, without looking up from the iPad. The light came through the wooden Chinese blinds, making his brown hair look golden.

When Peter woke up he looked like James Dean. I woke up looking like I had been in a bar-room brawl: matted hair, hunched over scrabbling for a lighter that still worked, my body feeling like it had been slammed against pavement.

When we walked down the street, I could hear people's thoughts, *Why is that handsome man with that scowling, smoking hag?* People would always ask me what was wrong. I must have looked pissed off all the time. People probably thought he was gay, and I was a fag hag secretly in love with him.

Women don't have trophy husbands the same way men have trophy wives. Men can be disgusting and walk into a party with a sexy bitch on their arm and feel like hot shit. But being a woman walking into a party with a handsome man on your arm, the only thing you feel is insecure.

When I imagined myself through Ogden's sixty-three-year-old eyes – my smooth, wrinkle-free skin, my long dark hair, my unsagging breasts, my flat stomach – I felt hot. Sometimes my hair fell over my eyes, and I grinned and looked up at him, and I loved being in my own skin.

Peter stared at me as I put my hair in a ponytail. 'Are you high?' he asked.

I shook my head no.

I lied to Peter because he didn't understand shit. He didn't understand how snorting a bag of dope didn't mean I would end up becoming a toothless, cracked-out skank or whatever clichéd Hollywood bullshit was implanted in his brain. When I tried explaining things to him, he would hear someone with a drug problem trying to rationalise their drug problem.

He made me feel like I was someone with a drug problem trying to rationalise her drug problem.

I'd been a chipper since I was eighteen. The trick was you never did it three days in a row. I knew enough junkies to know I had to stop for a while, because if I kept using, it would stop providing any relief and become one more problem.

He apologised.

I could tell by the way he touched my face he wanted to do it.

'I love you,' he said. His breath smelled like shit. His hand rubbed between my legs, and I made all the sounds, then his hand went over my tits, pinching the nipples, making them hard so it hurt when they rubbed against my rough thermal shirt.

He fucked me from behind. Felt like a baseball mitt, stretching. Inside, it was everywhere. Visualise it. Ugly, veiny thing beating in and out of softness, pinkness, perfectness. That's the attraction, a kind of ruining. I liked it hard.

He played with my clit while he fucked me from behind, and I came because I liked feeling like his bitch on all fours.

After I came I wanted to sleep, and he was taking forever. You couldn't say, 'I'm going to rest my eyes but feel free to keep going.' You couldn't say, 'Stop pulling my hair, it was cool at first but now it's just pissing me off.' You couldn't say, 'Are you bored? I'm a little bored.'

Please come already.

He sped up, pulled out. I turned on my back and lifted my shirt, and he came all over my tits and belly.

I loved how much Peter came. I loved being drenched in his come. I loved lying there in it. I rubbed it into my skin with my fingertips.

I felt warm, and I thought of going somewhere new. I wanted to see his same face with a new background behind his head.

He wiped my stomach with his boxers and threw his boxers into the hamper.

'You shouldn't go alone to the doctor tomorrow,' he said. 'I'll go with you. I'll be late to work. It's at four?'

'It's not a big deal,' I said. I ran my finger down his back, zooming around all the moles that had never been checked for cancer because Peter didn't have health insurance.

'You don't need to be there, sport,' I said. I called him 'sport' because he drank a protein shake every morning.

There was no doctor's appointment. I'd made it up. I was supposed to meet Ogden.

I lied all the time. Sometimes I lied so I didn't have to answer questions, like saying my father was still alive so I didn't have to talk about him dying. I regularly told people my father was white. Not because of some deep-seated issue with being Indian, but because I didn't know much about Indian culture, and I felt more American than anything else. I lied because it felt true. I said it to get off the hook for answering questions about why cows are sacred or whatever.

You can't help the truth, the mundane details that frame people's perceptions of who you are, like where you were born, what your father does for a living, how many siblings you have. In our lies we offer the world a presentation of how we would be if we had complete control over our existence. That's why it's so embarrassing to get caught in a lie. It offers a glimpse into how you want to be seen. *These are the things I am insecure about.* You take things off the table, clean up your stories, edit out the parts that don't make sense, and think, *Now that's better.*

I ran my hand through Peter's soft, sleepy hair. I lied to Peter about Ogden because I didn't want to hurt him. In a different world, maybe he would have understood that I was only trying to protect him. How if I didn't, I would drown him with my neediness and insecurities. Peter wasn't capable of helping me. He knew how to love, but he didn't know how to talk me through the layers of my neuroses.

'I don't wanna go to work today,' he whined, stretching.

Peter was a bartender at a high-end restaurant on the Upper West Side.

He must have casually mentioned 'my wife' in stories to customers at the bar. They'd imagine the kind of woman they thought a handsome, charming man like Peter would have as a wife. The character in the book never looks like the actor in the movie playing them.

I straddled him and kissed him as if I was paying a toll on my way over him. I picked up the seltzer from his bedside table and chugged it in front of the window.

'Put some clothes on. You can see everything through those blinds,' he said.

'Who cares? It's my apartment. What are they going to think? A woman is half-naked in her own apartment?'

Peter was always caring about things that didn't matter.

In the bathroom, I plucked hairs out of my upper lip with tweezers. I liked the feeling of the hair being pulled out of the follicles underneath the skin. Some of the hairs the tweezers could never grasp. I ended up drawing blood, and the hair was still right there. I rubbed the hairs off the tweezers onto my finger. The fat part like the top of a comma. I touched the ends with my fingers. Black and wiry.

Peter materialised in the bathroom mirror behind me like some kind of bizarro vampire. 'How long have you been lying to me?' he said. He took out exhibit A: a rolled dollar bill. 'I found this on the coffee table.'

I shrugged. 'That is a rolled bill. It is not a drug,' I said, high.

'Maya, c'mon. You don't have to lie to me.' He called me by my name when he was serious.

'Don't be serious,' I said, as if I didn't want to hear it.

'I'm not an idiot. Whatever. It's your life. I don't even know why I try –' And then he said more things. Things I didn't care to hear. Things that made me try hard to think of other things until he left and I could get more high and not think about anything.

Ogden never gave me shit. Ogden only listened.

The ways Ogden drove me insane were the ways I wanted to be exactly like him.

I wished Ogden could love me the way I loved him, but he never would, because I cared too much and was always opening up to him. Nobody wanted anyone who talked so easily about everything. They wanted a big puzzle and a goddamn treasure map. Find my heart by going through all these torture chambers. That's what people wanted: challenge and mystery. Poor Ogden. I was like, here are all my scars. I'll tell you my secrets as you die of boredom. Here are the answers to questions you never cared enough to ask. I lifted up my shirt and said, 'Please love me.' I lifted up my skirt and said, 'Please don't leave yet.' I felt empty when his cock wasn't in me. I wanted him to order me around. I wanted to be his personal come dumpster. I loved when his whole body was on top of me and his arms and legs surrounded me on all sides, like he was a big insect about to rip my head off.

When Ogden told me it was going to be okay, I believed him, because he was old and knew stuff about life that I didn't.

After Peter told me he loved me for the first time, I said, 'Peter, I am fucking crazy, and I will fuck this up.' And he nodded. Maybe he saw it as a challenge. Maybe he thought, *Well, at least this will be interesting.* But he kept coming over, and he kept watching me turn from sane person to insane person to sorry child, and then we'd hug, and I was forgiven. And so I had to ask myself, *Who was the crazier one?*

Peter and I met when we worked at the same bookstore. Peter's on-again, off-again girlfriend didn't show up to the store Christmas party. I played chess with him, and then we went back to my place. We talked on the couch. I went to the bathroom and shaved my pussy and thighs. When I walked back in, he was just standing there. We kissed. His beard itched my face. His pubic hair was wild. He put it in me without a condom. His necklace was swinging as he fucked me, so he flung it onto his back. He said, 'What do you want?' He had a cold so he sniffled as he fucked me. There was something sweet about the way he sniffled, like the whole thing already felt normal.

It felt as though Peter had followed me home one day and never left.

Sometimes men are like cabs with their lights on, and you just have to be there to pull them over.

Later he told me I hurt him that night. That he wanted to cuddle and he felt bad because I rolled over and went to sleep. He fell in love with how I didn't give a shit he was there.

'Don't move,' he said to me, when I was sitting naked in a chair. 'You look like a painting.'

We touched so much it didn't feel like someone else's skin.

In the beginning we listened to music and everything was new. Five years later, we watched television and everything felt old.

Peter hated me for not being there, and then he hated me for being there. I had to keep remembering he loved someone who didn't exist. As soon as he saw who I was, he would get the fuck away from me like any man in his right mind would. Ogden saw me for who I was, all the bad and all the good. He could keep it all in his mind and still wanted to fuck me.

Excerpt from conversation 12,983, Peter to me: 'You live like a homeless person indoors.'

Excerpt from conversation 20,939, Peter to me: 'You make me feel like an employee.'

Excerpt from conversation 56,543, Peter to me: 'You don't understand why it makes me feel bad that you asked me not to speak when Benedict Cumberbatch is on television?'

In the beginning, I wanted to put Peter in the right clothes. I wanted to dress him up, take him around, and then bring him home and say, 'Now take off your clothes and fuck me.' He wore brown, pleated corduroy pants, shirts with corporate logos, and sad brown shoes that his mother had bought him for Christmas. I put him in dark jeans, cool T-shirts, beaten flannels, and motorcycle boots.

If I divorced him, another woman would get him already fixed up.

After we got married, I encouraged (i.e., nagged) Peter to get a bartending job.

This was what Peter did when I tried to improve his life: he told me to leave him alone. A few days later he would say that after thinking about it he had come up with a plan, and his plan was exactly what I had told him to do. I couldn't say how it was my idea to begin with, or he wouldn't want to do it anymore.

Peter's parents were born-again Christians and brought him up in a renovated barn with no heat. For no conceivable reason, his mother didn't work. The kids were raised on the meager salary of his father, a preacher. His parents took pride in not collecting the welfare or food stamps they were doubtlessly eligible for. He was raised to believe that instead of being sad for what you don't have, you should be happy having nothing. Nothingness was close to godliness. I was sad for him that they didn't let him dream.

He saved change so he could buy a brand-new baseball cap. When he brought it home, his father yelled, 'Do you know how much food you could have bought?' When Peter told me this story, I said, 'Probably not very much.'

It broke my heart to think of this little kid who wanted a dumb baseball cap. Paging Dickens. It broke my heart again that his father had won – that he did break Peter in some fundamental way. Instead of teaching his son not to be brainwashed into thinking having things would ruin your life, he made his son believe he wasn't good enough to have things. Peter would always think the world was divided between those who were served and those who were servers. That was probably why he drank. Achieving anything was hard enough without someone kicking the dreaming out of you.

I'm not a psychologist, but I could be. It's not that hard to understand how people got all fucked up.

Peter showed up at an open call and got hired as a bartender on the spot. The guy who interviewed him was gay. Gay guys loved my husband. I used to think Peter was secretly gay and that gay guys could pick up on it, so I kept making jokes about him being gay, and then I tried to finger his ass when I blew him to see how he would react to penetration. He freaked out and told me he really wasn't gay and to stop trying to finger his ass. He seemed suspiciously angry, so I figured he still might be part gay.

Peter yelled 'I love you' through the bathroom door and left for work.

I got back in bed and bunched up the blanket and rubbed myself on it, but I must have fallen asleep before I came.

I woke up starving. I tried to love the hunger. I imagined the hunger was like the vibration you felt under your feet on a train. This hunger would lead to perfection: a face of cheekbones, hipbones sticking out, clavicles jutting. Light and empty.

Smart women are supposed to say certain things. You are supposed to say, 'I care about being healthy, not skinny.' Or '[Insert female celebrity] looked better when she wasn't so skinny. When she looked normal.' All women encourage one another to eat. They say, 'I'm so jealous of your curves,' as they think, 'Yeah, eat more, fatty.' I wanted nothing more than to be rail thin and say, 'It's so annoying. I eat so much and can't ever gain weight.'

I opened a peach Greek yogurt. I had been subsisting on yogurt for the last seven days. I was tired of eating things with the consistency of baby food. When you are not eating, you are scared of yourself. Scared you will accidently run out and buy a pizza. It's important to eat something so the hunger won't build to the point that you do something crazy, like buy a jar of peanut butter thinking one bite won't hurt, and then you're like, fuck it, and eat the whole thing. As soon as I ate a bite of the yogurt, I felt like a failure.

You are living on an average of 120 to 400 calories a day, and 800 calories a day is considered a starvation diet. You feel empty and light. You feel like a winner, above those losers who have to fill their hole three times a day and then complain they are fat. You have plenty of energy with nothing in your belly. It's terrifying how fast this becomes normal. You can't eat the peach ooze at the bottom.

The more you want to be free of food, the more obsessed you become with it.

Eating so little makes your taste buds restless. You crave salt, sugar, hot sauce, mustard, pickles. Your tongue wants to come out of retirement and be alive. Weird food combinations. Using a tomato to shovel spicy mustard into your mouth, and in between, a squeeze of honey. You are basically eating garbage.

Sometimes I felt like I was pushing against the day, and it wouldn't go anywhere. I sat in the chair. Dust particles in the light. I stared into the mirror. I lifted my shirt. I sucked in my stomach and thought, *This is how it would look.*

Sometimes I sat around and hated my body. I hated how when I got fat it was all in my belly, so I looked pregnant. I was top-heavy, with my belly, huge tits, and fatty armpits being carried by two stick legs. If I were a doll, I would be falling over constantly. My armpits were fat and stupid. I hated how my thighs touched on the toilet seat. I hated how these giant hairs came out of my neck, like, *Where the fuck did that come from?* How so much of my life was spent tweezing and shaving and waxing. My big, sloppy tits. When I ran to the bus it was a scene. I had no ass. It was like a disfigurement, how my back had this little bit of fat hanging with a split in it. I wanted to tear my tits off and stuff all the fat in my ass so I'd have one of those asses men could imagine slapping as they fucked it.

Ogden said, 'You're cute.' Cute meant you were a chubby girl with a nice face. All his exes were around my age and looked horse-faced and like they would never stop talking about boring things. If I were a guy, I wouldn't have fucked her with your dick. He probably thought it was great how dumb and boring women could be.

Ogden's ex wrote a memoir about her rich, boring life and her brief addiction to coke.

> 'Finally all the drug cliché memories, put in a blender and into one book.' —the *New York Times*

> 'Good for killing small bugs.' —the *Chicago Tribune*

> 'Another piece of garbage written by a privileged white woman with too much time on her hands, whom the world somehow has given the impression it gives a shit about her stupid life.' — *Everyone who has ever read it*

'Ogden, she sounds so boring I almost died,' I'd said to him after I read it. He stared at me blankly, and then said, 'Nah, she was great.' He really did think she was great.

It isn't fair how you can be this white girl with a busted face and you will be picked in the gym class of life before all the pretty brown girls. It doesn't matter how smart and cool you are. All these liberal cool guys who are all PC, but they only want to put their cock in white girls. They can be unfair with their love, and there isn't a damn thing you can about it.

The whole world wanted young white girls.

You have to play dumb. Guys like being smart and funny. If you want to compete with white girls, the least you can do is learn to laugh at jokes, not make them up. To ask lots of questions and not tell stories.

Sometimes I wondered if there was a correlation between how Peter always bought himself the crappy stuff and him choosing me: a thrifty, generic brown one, instead of name-brand white one with blond hair. He had rummaged through the bin and said, 'This brown one will do. It has all the same parts as the white one.' He liked things that were a little damaged or messed up. It gave him some kind of weird thrill. He mistook damage for having character.

Peter picked me, and I was throwing myself at an old man who would never ever pick me over a white girl. Sometimes when I was with Ogden, I thought too long about how Peter had really meant his vows, and a terrible feeling came over me that made my heart race. It was scary to have that kind of responsibility. I wished I could just fuck it up already and he would go. The idea of being totally faithful to Peter and trying my best to make it work filled me with dread and anxiety, because what would I hold on to if he left me? I knew deep down that Peter would leave me, so why would I stay faithful to him? Ogden was my safety net. Hopefully that meant I wouldn't hit the ground too hard when it all blew up in my face.

I woke up at 4:25. I had five minutes to get to work. I spent the first three with my face buried in a throw pillow. I spent the last two getting up and finding the dope. I did four lines just to get used to the idea of leaving the house.

I emptied the drawers looking for a T-shirt. You can never find the thing you're looking for.

I felt like a mess in a mess. What if I were forty and digging through the same pile of clothes, looking for the same T-shirt, with no family or friends left? Do some lives stop like that? Everyone leaves, and nothing else happens.

You think, *I only have this much time. I have to do important things.* But then you can't think of any important things.

I stared at myself in the mirror. What about this face made it mine? I scratched off an ice cream stain from my thermal. I felt a dread knotted in the back of my hair and ripped it apart. It was easy for everyone to wake up and shower and brush their teeth, but I lived between the days, so it was hard to know when to do these things.

The courtyard was a major selling point when I had come to see the apartment – large, grassy, with manicured rows of flowers and a few trees. The type of thing people in New York City made out to be a big deal. 'Wow, look at this.'

I bought the apartment with the money I had inherited when my father died.

My father had been thirty years older than my mom. He died at the age of ninety. I kept waiting to feel something after he died, like maybe there was some love stored up for him deep in my psyche, but the only tears that came were for my mother, who looked so gentle and broken at the funeral.

I felt bad for not feeling worse. People always talked about not getting over the death of a parent. When I said my father was dead, everyone was so sympathetic I felt like a fraud.

Before Peter, all my boyfriends had been older men. I suspected there was a father-sized hole inside me. I called Ogden 'Daddy' when he fucked me.

I loved Ogden's crow's feet. He walked fast and talked like Lou Reed. He smoked cigarettes, and instead of using an ashtray, he would leave half-smoked cigarettes standing upright on bookshelves. He was such a New Yorker, the way he talked about leaving New York all the time.

One time I saw Ogden ash on his jeans and wipe the ash into the material. He owned drills and saws, and picked up boxes of stuff and moved them around. I liked men who moved stuff around.

It was my mother's idea to buy the apartment. I loved it because it was old and cheap. Just like me one day. I didn't care that it was on the ground floor and received no light. I didn't care that it was far from the train. It was a cave. It was a womb. I didn't want one of those shiny, crappy, parquet-floored drywall apartments in those new, flimsy motel-looking buildings the broker kept showing me. My apartment had plaster walls. It was solid. It cost 250,000 dollars.

It was cheap because fifteen years ago, a man broke into the apartment across the hall and shot the elderly couple who were asleep there, and then broke into my apartment, drank a beer, jerked off to porn tapes, and shot himself. Later it came out his girlfriend had dumped him.

That dude was fucking nuts.

The broker told me they used to have real fish in the fountain, but then people in the building started abusing them (her words), and they had to get rid of the fish. She probably said this to me, a potential buyer, to illustrate how she knew every quirky detail of the building's eccentric history. But what she was actually relaying to her clients, and what I had to consider every time I passed that fountain, was that this was a building filled with people who would abuse fish if given the chance.

The day was dreary. I wore the weather like a torn shirt.

Grand Street was buzzing. The regular trio of weirdoes in front of the bodega. The girls with their gold chains and tight-ass jeans. Teenagers pushing strollers. A Hasidic woman in black with three yarmulked boys running ahead of her, their faces framed by ringlets. Like a Diane Arbus photo, two little girls, hand in hand, skipped down the sidewalk in perfect unison.

A white yuppie woman with a baby slung over her shoulder. The children looked like trophies. The women were mocking me, *Haha, we got a man to have a baby with us.*

I was pissed at Peter for not having a kid with me.

'My mom is so cool. She smokes pot with me, and she's always encouraging me to do whatever I want,' my future kid would say.

I would be one of those sick mothers who was fat and forever complaining. 'I spent my childhood taking care of my mother. She was always sending me to the store to buy two-liter bottles of Diet Coke with her disability checks,' my future kid would say.

Women with kids talk about how they are so busy and tired, but in their eyes they are saying, 'Envy me.' I did. I wanted to be so tired and busy.

If I believed in God, I would think he was waiting for me to get my shit together.

It didn't seem that long ago that I would freak out every time my period was late, running into the all-night pharmacy to pick up a pregnancy test and ending up in a girlfriend's bathroom, where we would chain-smoke and then gasp with relief when the plus didn't appear in the oval. And now every second week of the month, I was met with the familiar disappointment when confronted with the smear of blood on toilet paper. A marker of yet another thing not happening.

All those years imagining the horror of a screaming red-faced alien forcing its way out of me somehow morphed into the ultimate climatic conclusion of my biological longing. To lie there with a baby sucking on my nipple in a symbiotic bubble of warmth and love. To never be alone again. To have a reason to take care of myself. To love something more than myself. To have a clear and understandable answer to the question, 'So what do you do?'

I wanted to erase myself. Where there was a picture of me, there would be a picture of a snotty, pudgy infant, new to the world, with its tiny hand out, grasping at nothing. On my Facebook page, above my name, there would be his or her little face. Take the best of me, take this genetic line further, and then a little further, till the sky turns black and we freeze and we melt. We are all babies. We will always be babies. All the babies will die. And one day they will be dead forever. But it was nothing to get stuck on. It was nothing to get snagged on. Enjoy the rolling skies of your time-lapsed world: This was where you crawled out of the ocean, this was where you walked. That was where you were running, and then you were lying, and now you're looking up at the ceiling, and above the ceiling is the same sky that rolls ahead and will keep rolling on after you are gone. Say, 'Look at that.' Think, *I can do that.* Don't be scared. It will all be over long after no one remembers you.

When I was in India to scatter my father's ashes, I saw children just crawling around in the garbage. Probably just a matter of bribing the right person. Better that way – set the standard low.

So you could think, *At least you're not crawling around in the garbage,* if you ended up fucking up the kid's life somehow. But of course, you would never say that.

'What size is your shoe?' a hunched-over woman asked me. I thought of that film *The Conversation.* How everyone was once someone's child. Someone loved this woman once more than anything else in the world. Or maybe they didn't, and that's why she was fucked-up.

'Eight,' I said, looking down to avoid her stare.

'Looks bigger,' she said. Was she crazy or lonely? Crazy people could be lonely. Loneliness could drive you crazy.

I put my bus pass in the slot. The driver smiled at me. Hot black guy. He had a shaved head, and I could see how muscular his body was through his blue MTA shirt. I imagined lying flat on my belly. How he would spread my ass cheeks so he could get a good look at his cock going in and out of me. Take out all his aggression about his stupid life driving in circles. The smell of potato chips hit me as I walked toward the back of the bus and sat next to a window. Someone's headphones were too loud.

My phone was ringing.

'Have you heard back about your thesis?' my mother yelled into the phone.

'No.'

'You should email him.'

'It's only been three days since I turned it in.' This was a lie. I hadn't turned in the fucking thing. It was another cloud hanging over me.

'If you don't hear back by the end of the week –'

'I will, I will,' I said, regretting I'd picked up the phone.

'Did you read the story I sent you about the baby eagle in Mexico?'

'No, I didn't,' I said, feeling guilty I had deleted the article.

'There was this boy named Miguel,' she started.

The guilt instantly turned into annoyance. *Not now. Not now.* 'I'm on the bus,' I said, digging around for Chap Stick.

She kept saying, 'What?' and I kept screaming into the phone, 'I'm on the bus, Mom. I can't talk right now!' Why did the whole bus decide to be completely silent while I was on the phone? No teenagers laughing, no cell phones ringing, no mothers yelling at their kids not to touch the gum squished between the seat and the window. That feeling of embarrassment that fills you when you see people be mean to their parents. 'I can't talk to you! Because I'm on the bus!'

Finally she understood, but she took it as a piece of information, not as a reason to stop talking and get off the phone, because she wasn't a normal person. She was a mother. Her frontal lobe had come out with her placenta. 'So what day will you be coming up for your uncle's retirement party?'

This was a setup. She asked the question as if we had previously discussed it. When I told her I wasn't coming, she would act shocked and demand to know why, and then it was just a short hop and skip to the guilt trip, with a brief layover in Obligation City. These were our roles. This was our script.

'I can't come because I have to work.'

There was a pause. I was off script. She had to improvise.

'Why can't someone just cover your shift?' Pretty good.

'I asked, but nobody can.' Volley it back.

'It's just a bookstore! It's not like a real job.'

'Thanks. It's just my life!' A fat woman whom I hadn't known existed till that moment turned around to stare. It was as if God had put extras on a bus to remind me what a brat I was.

'When are you going to start sending out those applications for teaching?'

'I have to graduate first! God! I told you that!'

'Then if you turned in your thesis you need to bother them.'

'It's only been three fucking days!'

When I was a kid I brought home a picture from art class. My mother stared at it with a puzzled look and said, 'Trees aren't purple. What is wrong with you?' I watched it sway in the air before it landed in the garbage. On the fridge was a test my brother had gotten an A on. A concise little story that played well in therapy.

Before I was about to hang up self-righteously, she said, 'I've had trouble swallowing lately.' And just like that, she'd won. It didn't matter what she had ever done to me. She was sick, and she was my mom. Emotional kryptonite. The lump in my throat. With a snap of her fingers she could turn me into a lost six-year-old with tears running down my face, just wanting my mommy. Somehow that's what happens when you deal with the very first person you met on Earth.

I stared out of the messed-up bus window at a drunk taking a piss. This dirty town. 'I don't know where all this mucus comes from,' she said. I listened with an overwhelming sense of fear and dread as she told me all the fucked-up things her body was doing.

It doesn't matter how old you are, after your mom dies you will still feel like an orphan, out there completely alone in the world.

You always feel like a champ when you make your mom laugh.

I picked shreds of tobacco from the Chap Stick, listening to my mother. I found myself saying, 'I would come, but I have a lot going on right now.'

I loved my mother. I felt bad that she wanted to love me, but she did all the exact wrong things. I felt bad she could be so cruel, like when she threw in my face that I went to a shrink, as if that gave her the authority of the sane, and dismissed all my grievances. Not that it was her fault. Nothing was her fault. It was the way she was raised. She had my brother when she was just nineteen years old; like, what did she fucking know about anything? She'd never lived on her own. She went from her parent's house to her husband's house. *Her husband.* He wasn't easy. She was so bright and crafty, and she could have lived a whole life and not just been a glorified servant. Who could blame her for being nuts? Her father and her husband had deprived her of being a person. She was raised to believe the best thing to be was a wife and mother. It was so sad. And we were so hard on her. What do you do when your teenage daughter tells you she wants to die? When she cries and screams and disappears for days? What would you do? What would I do?

My brother told me there was a chair in her shower now. It was the saddest thing I could imagine.

Indians are always cremated. The body that grew from a baby into my mother would go into the oven and turn to ash with bits of bone.

It's important to drink milk because calcium is what bones are made of.

Her ashes would go where my father's had gone: The dark cloudy waters of the Ganges. Where sick people bathe. Where there is someone pissing, someone shitting, and someone vomiting right now. And then my brother. And then, finally, me, the baby of the family, the last one to be dumped in the water, forgotten and dead, just like everyone else.

We would be dead, so we wouldn't care how disgusting the water was.

It took all the way from Fourteenth and Fifth down to Astor Place to shake off the guilty feelings.

I walked into Starbucks. I was always late to work. But after that phone call, I deserved a treat. A skinny caramel latte was 100 calories. But I needed all the sugar and caffeine and fat of a mocha frap, with a big fat unnecessary swirl of whipped cream on top, because death is serious business.

All the women in Starbucks were wearing cardigans. All the women of fuckable age, anyway. It was as if someone from wardrobe had come in with a rack of cardigans, and each of the women selected one. There's this moment in New York City when all the women are wearing different versions of the same thing, as if they all had gotten a memo, and you have to decide, *Am I going to join this trend?*

If you don't get on board, you will feel like an out-of-touch loser (NYC is like high school: trends, being judgmental, and how impressive it is when you find out someone has a car – *Really? You have a car.* But if you do go with the trend, you will feel like a poser, no matter how much you actually like the scarf or skirt or whatever it is. Everyone who passes you will think you are just another follower. Loser or poser?

I walked into the bookstore at a casual pace, sipping my drink, chewing on the straw lackadaisically as I did not rush down the stairs.

'Jeez, don't you ever take a break?' I asked Ethan, who was sitting with his legs up on the receiving table with his eyes closed.

'I'm afraid of intimacy so I bury myself in work,' he said, not opening his eyes.

On Ethan's computer was a website of old men who looked like lesbians. Keith Richards. Elton John. Al Franken.

Justine came out of nowhere, like a ninja. 'My ass hurts,' she said.

'Why's that?' I asked, drawing a stick figure on the info table with black marker.

'I got fucked in the ass last night,' she said.

Justine and I hung out, but we weren't *The Sisterhood of the Traveling Pants*-type BFFs.

Justine's moment of glory was when this middle-aged woman had asked how the books were arranged, and Justine sang the alphabet at the top of her lungs.

Justine labeled the stapler, 'Lady Chatterley's stapler.'

Before I worked there, former employees had scrawled labels on the reshel-ving carts, 'Who carted?' 'Miss Lonelycarts,' and 'O brother, where cart thou.'

Justine told me, Ethan, and Mark about this piece of art that just sold for millions of dollars. You fed it food, and it turned it into shit. 'I've been eating and shitting for free all these years like a sucker!' Ethan joked. Mark asked what would happen if you fed shit to it. Ethan said you would get more shit.

'Like the same amount of shit or twice the amount of shit?' I asked. Everyone laughed.

I gave the stick figure a hand and put a gun in it.

'Maya,' Michelle said. 'So I don't know if you've heard, but they're sending someone to take over the textbook department.' Michelle was the general manager. She grinned as she clapped her hands silently. I smiled back. She went on, 'They're going to expand this whole section. The counter will come out to here.' I didn't look up to see where she was indicating because I didn't give a shit.

'You must be happy you don't have to deal with textbooks anymore,' I said, slurping melted ice.

'I've worked my ass off at this store, and now all the burden and hassle of textbooks will be off my shoulders. I can finally make the store what I always wanted it to be. We can have readings!' she said, beaming and exposing her yellowed, plaque-laden front teeth. Michelle in her fuzzy sweaters, with her cozy beer gut and her slowly rotting teeth.

'Wow,' I said, trying to sound like I cared. My high was wearing off. My nose was a faucet that wouldn't stop. I wiped snot on my sleeve.

'Listen, I have to go meet John for dinner,' Michelle said.

'Someplace fancy?' I asked. I wondered if it was obvious how much I didn't care.

'We're celebrating. He got a promotion.'

'What does he do, again?'

'He does the same thing as Pete does on *Mad Men*,' she said, sounding as if she had used that line several times before.

Michelle had graduated from NYU, majoring in English, and she would work at this shitty job until she started having babies with her fat husband, and no one would wonder why she looked like shit.

When you're a fat girl and you make an effort with your clothes and hair, it's like, why bother, you're still fat. Like you're saying to the world you're content with being fat. But if you just throw on sweatpants, you are this fat girl walking around in sweatpants. Have some self-respect. You can't win.

After Michelle left, my withdrawals got worse. I was left alone in textbooks. I called up to Mark at the register.

'I have to take a huge dump.'

'Okay, why are you announcing that to the store?' There was laughter. I heard someone clap.

'What?'

'Take your finger off the intercom button.'

I took my finger off it. 'I thought it was a one, not an *I*.'

'*I* is for intercom. How long have you worked here?'

'I was born in fiction and raised in science fiction.'

'I'll be down in a second to cover for you.'

Afterwards I stood frozen in front of the toilet, trying to figure out what to do. The toilet had problems flushing, and I had taken the biggest dump I had ever seen. I was simultaneously embarrassed it came out of me and fascinated by how weird my body could be. If only I could cut it up into pieces to make it easier for the toilet to, like, digest it. I looked around the toilet for something I could MacGyver together. There was a generic air freshener that made the shit smell worse by layering a waft of mint on top, sort of like how it's somehow dirtier to wear crotchless panties than to just be naked. I took the toilet brush and stabbed the shit. I ended up getting shit all over the brush and splashing some of the shitty water onto my sleeve. I was scared that if I kept at it I would end up with shit water on my face and spend the rest of my life scrubbing my face off. I put the shitty brush behind the toilet. No one would know it was me. People see shit, and they think of dudes.

'Don't tell anyone about the intercom,' I said.

'I wouldn't, Maya. C'mon,' Mark said. Mark was rail thin. He was Chinese American. Generations of his family had lived in California. There was a hint of surfer dude accent in his voice. He was so small. Whenever I imagined myself doing him, I thought of a fat brown cow sitting on a beautiful little dove.

'I don't feel well.' My neck was sweating.

'If you want to go in half an hour, I don't mind closing without you.'

'Mark, you're too good to me.'

'I'm too nice. That's why I don't have a girlfriend.'

'No, that's not it. It's your clothes. Oh, and your personality and face.'

'Right. I forgot about those things.'

'Actually, you have a nice face.'

Awkward silence.

'Thanks, Maya.'

'I mean, not for me, but for, like, the world or whatever.'

'Yeah, I know what you mean.' He smiled. He was so sweet. I was a tease.

Mark went back upstairs, and I was alone. No one came downstairs after about seven or so. Only nonfiction and plays were downstairs. I picked up *Fun Home,* this graphic novel I was reading, but my eyes kept tearing up.

My head was buzzing, and I felt dizzy. I thought of fucking Ogden to distract myself.

I thought of how I was going to say, 'Yeah, fuck me, Daddy,' as he pounded me from behind.

I thought of how when he fucked me missionary, he pulled down the cups of my bra so my tits spilled out.

For an old dude, Ogden had a nice body. He was thin but muscular. He had a few white hairs on his chest and belly. He was tall. When he was fucking me on the edge of the bed, I liked putting my hand out and feeling his stomach. I liked how it was hard and fuzzy, and how there was no fat there. You couldn't tell he was old till you scanned back up and looked at his face. Or his ass. He had an old, droopy, sad ass. Most men have sad asses, but Peter didn't. Peter had a robust, taut booty that stuck out. I didn't understand why women like men's butts, like how they showed women checking them out in movies.

One time Ogden fingered my ass as he fucked my mouth. I was on all fours on the bed, and he was standing. I pulled back too far, and his cock fell out of my mouth. 'C'mon,' he said, and put his cock back into mouth. I liked feeling like a thing.

I liked feeling like nothing.

There was more nothing in a woman. There were the asshole, pussy, and mouth. But you could also store a baby in the belly and two jugs of milk fit perfectly in each tit.

Imagine the voice-over in a car commercial, and the image of a woman's naked body on a shiny black surface, the camera slowly panning up. *The female body, luxurious and roomy, can accommodate three cocks and three babies at full capacity. One baby sucking on each nipple and one sleeping comfortably inside* [show ultrasound of zygote in women's belly] *while there is one cock in the pussy, one in the ass, and one sliding in and out of the mouth.*

I imagined being tied to a bed and different men coming in and fucking me.

I was pouring sweat. I was horny and felt gross. The slicks of sweat gathered underneath my tits. My high school best friend, Molly, used to say belly buttons smelled like hot dogs. I wanted to take a long shower, brush my teeth, buy a cardigan, and be a normal human fucking being.

I thought about a man pushing my head down so my forehead pressed against the counter as he fucked me from behind.

I went on Facebook and found this guy Ian I knew from high school. He used be hot and wore T-shirts of cool bands you were embarrassed to say you'd never heard of. He had gotten fat, and his status updates were about the food he cooked. 'Made vegetable fajitas with peppers, tomatoes, onions from the farmer's market, avocados, and Mexican cheese, wrapped in a homemade tortilla.' And then there was a picture of what looked like sad brown food covered in a fat scoop of sour cream on a terra cotta plate. Why did seventeen people like this? Why did some girl named Terry need the recipe to make it for 'her hubby'?

The word 'hubby' made me cringe.

Molly was on Gchat.

Maya: what's with Ian's posts everyday about
what he eats?

Molly: jesus, I know. he's always making quinoa
and then covering it in a tub of cheese

Maya: he's getting fatter and fatter

Molly: yeah, he's probably eating a box of
donuts right now covered with a box of
donuts

Maya: remember when I stole his sock for you?
you were obsessed

Molly: gawd, I hate time. he used to be so
fucking hot and now he's like the worst bitch
ever. remember his hair?

Maya: how's nathan?

8:35 PM

Molly: I'm in post sex cloud of clouds

Maya: you're still hooking up with him?

8:36 PM

Molly: i couldn't walk straight when i left his
house today. he found a way to bang
straight into my g spot for like a thousand
years. i went cross eyed. this would be the
highlight of any fat mom's life.

8:38 PM

that's probably TMI. sorry.

Maya: no it's awesome

8:39 PM

Molly: yeah. it kind of freaks me out that we aren't done figuring out what to do with each other's bodies yet. i predict at least another year until this shit wears off.

8:40 PM

i'm sorry. it's boring.

8:42 PM

Maya: i'm supposed to see ogden tomorrow

Molly: !!!

Maya: it's so over

Molly: why do you think that?

Maya: he's making me feel like shit all the time. i feel like he hates me. he really likes anal. do you think that means he's like 2 steps closer to gay on the kinsey scale or a misogynist?

Molly: misogynist. Oh god. did I tell you I think nathan does that thing where he hangs himself when he jerks off?

8:44 PM

Maya: like David carridine?

8:45 PM

Molly: there's a rope in his bathroom but i'm scared to ask cuz i don't wanna embarrass him. yesterday was nathan's birthday. he's 39. i'm in love with his forearms. hopeless case over here! good lord that was intense today. what's a girl to do? just float around on it when it exists, i guess.

8:52 PM

i need to smoke hash and watch tv now.

8:53 PM

maybe i'm a nympho. do you think there are
  other women out there who would make
  such a big deal out of fucking?
8:55 PM
Maya: yeah, fucking is universally and
  historically something people make a big
  deal out of. love, fucking, and art. do you
  still ever paint? i still have that one you gave
  me for my birthday somewhere. it was really
  good.
8:56 PM
Molly: boo. i was never talented. i didn't care so
  i was like free or whatever. having a kid has
  made me boring and fat and i can't even
  enjoy this nathan thing cuz i don't know how
  to be the kind of person who doesn't care if
  it goes away or not. i'm in an old lady panic
  about it.
8:58 PM
the sex got better last month. by a mile. he used
  to be really selfish and weird in bed, which
  i just happen to think is hot. but now, i'm
  having like black out fireworks stuff
Maya: i'm so jealous. last time ogden didn't
  even want to
9:01 PM
Molly: the same thing happened with me and
  nathan where we didn't fuck for a while and i
  thought maybe that was the end, so i asked
  him over email 'do you think we are winding
  down?'

and he just said 'i'll wind you down.'

oh don't be jealous

i have a kid so i have to feel like i'm doing
     something wrong all the time. at least your
     life is still your own to fuck up.

[/message dialogue]

When I got out of the store, the cool air felt good on my hot skin. My hoodie was getting wet. I smelled rank. I broke into a run. Passed the couples, dodging umbrellas. Excuse me, excuse me, excuse me.

Fall off the Earth. Get high and think about how you should stop getting high.

My life was my own to fuck up. At least in America where you know you're free.

When I was kid, I was always on airplanes. I was an army brat, so we moved a lot. I would imagine how if the plane crashed others would be saved before me. I imagined the frustration rising up in me. Wanting to shout, 'Do you have any idea who I am?' There would be no way to tell them I was special. That I knew somehow I was destined for greatness. I thought it would be a misunderstanding if I died.

But then you grow up, and all the extras are real people. Like when you look down from a bridge and have to wrap your mind around how in each little toy car is a real person with a whole life. There are smart people everywhere. There are idiots everywhere. There is no order to it. There is no reason you're not dying in a cancer ward and some little kid is.

Ran up Elizabeth's stoop. I could hear the rats rustling just out of my peripheral vision. After I buzzed Elizabeth, I turned back and made myself stare at the rats bursting out of the garbage. Some were going into the hole in the garbage bag while other rats were running out, their skin touching as they passed one another. It made me jumpy, like one was about to run up my leg. Rats had teeth.

Molly once told me that her friend had a male rat, and when it went down her arm she could feel the rat's balls on her skin.

All Elizabeth's furniture had been found on the street or looked as though it had. The sofa had a maroon velvet sheet with black roses on it that was always sliding off. There was a sticker on the mirror of the medicine cabinet in the bathroom that read, 'Fuck You I'm Batman.' Noah, her ex, had his paintings hung up on the wall because he didn't have the money to put them in storage. Or so he claimed. She had dumped him nearly two years ago. There was something sinister about the way he left his stuff around. It was probably some kind of male territory type thing, like, 'My shit is here so this bitch is still mine.'

Noah's paintings were creepy. They looked like what would happen if Norman Rockwell were possessed by Charles Manson. They featured adolescent boys wearing white briefs and disturbing white masks with horns or snouts. A lot of the scenes were in nature. There was one of a little girl stabbing a giant fuzzy panda, and blood poured out of the wound and spattered her long dress.

You live in New York, and you're so cool. You have an apartment in the East Village, and you call yourself an artist. But after a while, you forget what it was you were so excited about. There is nothing here for you. You feel like a sucker every day paying fourteen bucks for a pack of smokes. You take stock of your resources, and you don't have anything. You call yourself an artist, but you work fifty million hours a week just to sleep in a room where only a bed fits. You go to bars where you can't sit down or hear anyone talk. You're a hipster in New York City. There are a million of you, and it doesn't matter that you believe you're talented, because no one cares and you're only getting older. The thing you didn't realise when you were fourteen and thought Kurt Cobain was God was that not every weirdo with an ironic tee from Urban Outfitters makes it. There are a lot of people in their sixties, toothless, broken, and poor, who have stories of almost making it. At what point do people hear 'loser' when you say 'artist'?

I didn't care how amazingly successful you got as long as you weren't younger than me.

The first thing Elizabeth did after opening the door was shush me. Not a good sign. She pointed through her railroad apartment to the bedroom, where I could make out two sleeping bodies. 'Noah and Candy,' she told me. I didn't know who Candy was.

I was disappointed she had let Noah in and into her bed, where he was probably crashing from whatever drug he had injected or smoked. That didn't bode well for Elizabeth's sobriety. Said me, the girl who was fiending for a bag of heroin, but hey, you still had those feelings. A year into Elizabeth's relationship with Noah, he lost his job and started smoking crack. I didn't know which had come first, losing his job or smoking crack, but my money was on the crack. He pretended to go to work every morning but instead went to his studio where he smoked crack and fucked around. He claimed he was taking care of the bills. But it all came out when Elizabeth started getting bills with bright red 'Final Notice' warnings. Elizabeth's mother paid all the back debt. Noah had helped Elizabeth clean up when they first met, so he laid a guilt trip on her when she tried kicking him out. And then he got her hooked on dope again, so she couldn't really get away. But she didn't blame him. She said, 'I'm an adult. No one can make you do anything.'

'Shit,' was the first thing Noah said when he came into the kitchen.

Noah owned a lot of scarves.

Five years of hardcore drug use had taken a heavy toll on him. The whole time they were together, he seemed frozen at twenty-five, but now he looked like he was pushing forty. It was weird how age didn't work in steady steps but was like a car accident: it hit you one day and left you fucked-up forever.

Noah took a jar of organic peanut butter out of the cabinet. He scooped some on his finger. The jar fell out of his hand and broke into pieces. He picked up a shard of the jar and wiped the peanut butter onto a piece of bread.

Noah's teeth were black and broke off in his sleep. Junkies don't brush. Don't ask me why. I don't know why.

Noah had contracted Hep. C. from all the injectables. When I asked Elizabeth what she thought would happen to him, she said these words like they were no big deal, 'He's going to die.'

Candy couldn't find her pills. She dumped her purse on the bed. Losing drugs makes you crazy. You alternate between, 'It has to be here' and 'I am going to be sick really soon, and there's nothing I can do to help it.'

Candy cornered Elizabeth and tried to pull the 'Maybe you accidently somehow ...' Elizabeth rolled her eyes. Candy was screaming at Noah to get off his ass and help her. Noah's eyes kept closing. I figured it out. Noah had stolen Candy's Xanax.

Elizabeth came out from the bedroom and said, 'Can you guys leave? You were supposed to come over for dinner and that was twenty-two hours ago.' And then she went back to the bedroom. I snotted on my sleeve. My head ached. Everything was raw, and dread filled me. The back of my head and neck were sweaty. Sometimes I was so desperate for drugs it was hard to act casual, which was the way we all tried to be. Like we were just using this one last time, and we didn't even care much about doing it. You have to pretend. That's why dealers are better. You don't have to pretend anything. Both of you just want your shit and to get the fuck away from each other as quickly as possible.

'I can get more tomorrow,' Noah said.

'Get it now,' Candy said.

'He isn't around now. We'll go to my place and then in the morning ...'

'Your place is gross,' she said.

'I can get you crack.'

'Do I look like a crackhead?' she shouted.

'I'm just telling you what I can get,' he mumbled.

You watch them. It's depressing. You want to run and never touch it again. Thank your lucky stars you never got caught, not even that one time you copped on Delancey Street in broad fucking daylight with cars whizzing by.

This little jail is made out of powder.

There is this powder people snort or shoot into their bodies that makes them feel good, but they end up turning into zombies, lying around, wasting their lives, getting older, and doing nothing. It makes you feel so good. It is a bad sci-fi movie, and you've seen that movie and how.

'You can shut the door,' Elizabeth said as I walked into the bedroom.

'Here.' She handed me a methadone pill. *Thank you, Elizabeth, for being so fucking considerate. You didn't make me have to act nice.*

'How much should I take?'

'What's your habit like?' she asked. The way she was wearing her reading glasses, I felt like we were at CVS, and she was the pharmacist.

'About a bag and a half a day for the last ten days,' I told her.

'If you want enough not to be dope sick, half is fine. If you want to get a high then take the whole pill.'

'Do you want money?'

'Nah, it's cool. They're only three bucks a pill,' she said. Was it even a crime if you didn't pay for it? Was the crime taking the drug or having it on you? Did New York City consider my body a container?

Elizabeth chased the dragon, lighting it off aluminum foil. She must waste a lot that way because the smoke goes everywhere. I wondered why people didn't use a bong or something to catch the smoke.

Elizabeth cleaned in red heels. Give that girl a bag of dope and watch everything sparkle. As she folded her size zero jeans, she told me Candy's story.

Candy lived Upstate. She and Noah had been friends when they worked at an art gallery together like ten years ago. She had gotten married, moved, and had two kids. Some dude had wanted to spend the rest of his life with that annoying bitch.

She friended Noah on Facebook.

Facebook: The way to ruin nice memories by having to meet up with people you should just be allowed to wonder what had happened to.

Candy was pretty hot in a vulgar, All-American, skanky way. Blond hair, vacant eyes. She had that vibe, like you could do whatever you wanted to her. Just bend her over. Like she was used to it. Like she'd been fucked so many times she wouldn't care if you had a turn. I kind of wished I could give off that vibe. Sometimes I tried, but it was always awkward. Something about me wasn't easy. Whatever it was made it harder for men to forget I was a real person. Every time I fucked someone it became complicated.

At some point Candy got addicted to pain pills. Her husband was leaving her. He was going to take the kids. She had to get clean. She asked Noah if he would look after her kids while she kicked if she came to the city and picked him up. And for whatever fucking reason, probably because he was high out of his mind, he agreed. Then Candy came down and put the large, simple pieces together. Noah brought her to an apartment that looked like a junkie lived there. There was a girl nodding out with an extension cord around her neck, who woke up and asked Candy if she was interested in buying an extension cord. Noah said he would be gone a few minutes but was gone for hours. There was no power. She sat in the dark and saw mice brazenly run across the counters. Noah finally came home, and she went off on him. He brought her to Elizabeth's to calm her down. After they ate, Noah started this shit with wanting to go and get clean with her. 'They just keep going back and forth about it. She'll be like 'I'm going by myself.' And then Noah will be like, 'I agreed to help you and I want to.' Then she cries. It never ends.' Elizabeth rolled her eyes. 'They won't fucking leave.'

'All I can imagine is babies wailing, and Noah and Candy passed out on the floor with lit cigarettes in their mouths and the stove on,' I said.

'Men our age are giant pussies,' Elizabeth said. 'I need a real man. Like an old-school dude who won't put up with my bullshit, you know? Someone who can take control of my life.'

'Yeah, I know,' I said, pouring the dope out of the bag she gave me onto a copy of *The Rum Diaries*.

Lying on the bed. Giggling, on our bellies, swinging our feet. We were two girls at camp. She said, 'Oh, Maya, when will we be swans?'

Elizabeth's clavicles were pronounced. She had long dark hair. She could have been a model. Sometimes I wanted to touch her stomach because it was perfect, how flat it was. Her shirts hung flawlessly because nothing was there to push them out. Men fell in love with her. Men followed her down the street trying to guess her name, like in a movie.

She always dated men who were losers and assholes.

Haven't you, haven't you seen it all before?

I was in love with Elizabeth. I wished we could be together, cooking, laughing, talking. I didn't want to have sex with her. I just always wanted to be with her, and to hear her laugh at my jokes and protect her. Or I wanted her flat stomach and size zero jeans and low-affect attitude, as if nothing could fuck with her. Elizabeth would not cry in a grocery store if her sixty-year-old boyfriend didn't pick up her phone call. Or maybe I did want to have sex with her. Who knew.

Elizabeth had lost her father very young. He was diagnosed with lung cancer when he was thirty-six, and she was seven. In her living room, there had been a hospital bed with a machine attached to him that gave him chemo. The cancer spread to his brain. No one told him he was dying. Elizabeth's mother told her not to tell him. The very last time she saw him, on his deathbed, he tried calling his office to tell his boss he couldn't come in. When she hugged him, he whispered to her that he would take her to the beach for her birthday.

After her father died, Elizabeth's mother assumed her husband's four brothers who lived close by would help out, but they didn't even come by, let alone lend her money. She was a middle-aged woman with two kids and she had never worked. Overnight her life resembled nothing she could have imagined. She was a widow with bills to pay. She drove Elizabeth in circles all night, crying and cursing her dead husband and his family.

Elizabeth went to eleven different schools. Her mother-packed lunch was always the same: a small can of tuna, a plastic fork, a V8, and one of those little red balls of cheese. 'I was the girl who smelled like tuna,' Elizabeth said with a smile.

At seventeen her mother bought her a one-way ticket to Boston. In Boston she lived in a house with other runaways and drug addicts. She got a job bartending. She tried heroin for the first time. Then she made her way to New York.

Elizabeth was always telling me her plans. She was always on the verge of getting clean. Then she would go into the bathroom, where Noah would shoot dope into her arm and her slight body would slump over, and then I would hear the obligatory toilet flush, as if anyone thought she was actually using the toilet. But she had been doing dope in secret for so long it was part of the routine.

I used dope to feel good. Elizabeth used it to feel nothing. She used till the money was gone. She would vomit in the toilet, pass out on the floor, wake up, and do more. She told me once, 'Since my dad died, I don't care about being alive.' She mixed pills and dope and drank on top of it. She wanted oblivion, she said, and death would only be a welcome side effect on the way to her goal. How her ninety-pound body could handle it all was a mystery. How she was able to maintain a job, working ten- to twelve-hour days as an editor for a magazine, was also a mystery, but it was mostly a curse. She was stuck in the cycle of making money to blow on her habit and needing dope to sustain the long hours of tedious work. She always was saying if she only made this much more then everything would be fine. But she would always need more money, no matter how much she made, because that was the nature of the problem, and the problem would never be solved as long as she could make money or maintain her job. There was nothing to throw a wrench in the cycle, no free time to offer a moment of clarity. Where was bottom? She worked high up in a building, and then she went home to her ground-floor apartment and shot all the money in her arm to feel nothing at all.

There used to be this D.A.R.E. commercial where this woman walked in a circle and kept muttering, 'I have to do drugs so I can work so I can make money so I can do drugs so I can work ...'

Where the fuck was bottom?

Elizabeth thought it was bullshit that I complained about my father. 'At least you had him growing up,' she said. There are no competitions for pain because no one can be objective. We all have our own private hells. Mine was a father who showed no interest in my existence. That's a hard problem to have because the precise problem is the absence of problems.

When I was a kid, I literally thought his name was 'Dad.'

But then I asked myself, *Who would I be if my father was a great dad?* What if what drove us – our sexual habits, our ambitions, our talents – all stemmed from someone not hugging us when we were kids? The best parts of us developed from overcompensating for something we weren't given. They say ugly girls have to develop a personality. Whatever hole was made when we were kids is the same size as our ambition and need for attention. So is it better to be interesting but damaged, or mediocre but stable? At NYU there were students with parents who were so encouraging it seemed to verge on another type of abuse, giving their children unfounded confidence in anything they put their sticky hands on for five minutes. This one girl told me how her parents had her read her stories during dinner, and they would all applaud.

My parents had thought I was an idiot. They had treated my interest in writing as a symptom of my failure to grasp reality. 'You're so smart, you could have gotten an MBA,' my mother said.

There was a knock. Elizabeth opened the door, and Noah stuck his head in. 'All right, I'm going to go get some crack. You want some?'

'Here,' Elizabeth said, handing him a fifty.

'My kids are everything to me,' Candy said for the millionth time. 'They are the whole reason I'm alive.' Then, 'You have beautiful hair.' She was so skanky. Someone should have put a cock in her mouth, if only to shut her up. But she probably wouldn't. She would probably babble some incoherent shit even while you fucked her. I wanted to throw up.

'I need to lie down,' I said to no one. I went back to the bedroom, crashed on the bed.

Fuck dope. Methadone is the new frontier. Only three bucks a pill. I leaned back against the wall. Hole up in the apartment. Should just stay good and fucked-up. Get real junkie skinny lying with my lovely hipbones sticking out of my dirty jeans. Some man I don't even know yet can curve his hand into my pants. Stay wet all the time. Read all I want in my room without having to think of dumb things to say about it. When I'm king. Jump in the ocean. Let the water go up my nose, I don't care. Drive Upstate with the windows down. Go fuck in a little tent. Pull weeds out of the ground. Drink beer. Pick at the label. Go for a drive. Park on the side of the road. Stare at the stars.

I woke up with dried drool all over my mouth and a craving for chocolate ice cream.

Elizabeth was lying next to me with her eyes closed, a lit cigarette between her lips. Night of the living dead. I took the cigarette and put it out.

'It's been real,' I said as I passed Candy taking a piss on the toilet. She gave me a Courtney Love face, half-closed eyes with a lipstick smear.

High. Walked down the street like I had a cock. Like the city was my bitch, and I was fucking it in the ass. *You're mine, you're mine, you're mine.*

I walked into the front door, and it slammed behind me. The apartment was quiet and dark. I had managed to walk past a million bodegas. Big crinkly bags of kettle chips and chocolate fudge brownie ice cream. The only thing at home was peach yogurt.

I went back out to the bodega. *Just to look,* I thought. Maybe a candy bar. Something that wouldn't make me feel guilty. I tried hard to remember the envy I felt staring at Elizabeth's beautiful, tiny thighs. How her body looked so perfect and clean, and mine looked sloppy and messy. I always thought I was doing okay until I spent time around her and realised I was nowhere close to being thin.

It was smarter to buy a pint of ice cream, but I knew what started as a few spoonfuls would end with an empty pint and a sick feeling. There were granola bars with chocolate chips and peanut butter. The thought of more granola … I knew this was dangerous territory, and this could spiral into a need for a treat every night, then pints of ice cream every day, and it would be gross.

I bought a Snicker's ice cream bar. The chocolate broke into pieces and released the creamy vanilla ice cream. There was nougat and the swirl of caramel. The first taste was a dull sensation of sugar. At first you think, *What's all the fuss about?* But then you find yourself wanting to go back and remember all the tastes: the salty nuts, the white cream, the thick caramel, the soft nougat, all mixed together. What exactly was nougat?

They should have girls with eating disorders do commercials for food.

I ate all but one bite and threw it in the garbage. There was a strong desire to take it right back out of the garbage and finish it.

I found my phone, but it was dead. I found a charger, but then I realised it was Peter's. So where's mine? All this technology, and you end up like a caveman, hunched over, trying to figure out what plugs into what.

If I called Ogden, he would be pissed off. It pissed him off to hear about my feelings. He kept me chained a million miles from his heart, and when I cried, he thought, *See, this is why I keep her chained so far away.*

He could be cold as fuck. Sometimes I cried and his eyes turned to these points of endless apathy, like, 'Go ahead and fucking die.'

Peter was too stupid to take care of me, and Ogden was too fucked-up. I would be middle-aged soon, and who in the world wanted to be with a middle-aged woman?

I called Ogden. He didn't pick up. The blurry images of him with another girl. A blurry girl with long brown hair and fresh white skin and tits with huge areolas. Opening her legs. I kept calling. I cried into his voicemail. I shouted into his voicemail. I sounded like a child. I sounded like someone you might not want to call back right away. Where is a good emergency when you actually need one?

When men stop wanting to fuck you: Poof! You disappear.

I took three Xanaxes and watched *Bob's Burger's* on my laptop till I passed out on the couch.

—

'We're going to be late,' Peter said. It was twenty past seven. We had to be at Penn Station at eight.

'It's not going to take forty minutes in a cab,' I said.

'There are no cabs.'

'There'll be one, just wait.' The wind blew in my face. My head hurt. Why did I ever agree to go to his parent's house for Thanksgiving? I cursed the past me, the one who hadn't considered what the present me would have to go through.

The past me was always fucking with the present me. Like agreeing to go jogging at nine in the morning, like agreeing to help people move, like making doctor's appointments at eight o'clock. Thinking naively, 'It will be good for me to start the day early.' But when the day finally arrived for whatever, that past me with too-high expectations for myself had totally fucked present me.

The psychiatrist had given me Suboxone. Suboxone was the new methadone. Like methadone it blocked dope, but Suboxone took longer to leave your system. You could see people nodding outside methadone clinics. Suboxone never did that. It didn't give you a real high like methadone, but it was something. It felt like you had drunk an entire pot of coffee and then took some shitty speed.

'Maya,' Peter started, but then a yellow cab with lights on turned the corner and I was saved from whatever tangent he was about to go on.

I slid into the seat, put my headphones on, and turned up the music. It was some indie band, singing, 'Everything's a mess,' and then something about a heart, and then I couldn't understand the words. Peter put our bags in the trunk and slammed the door a little too hard.

Penn Station was packed. Kids twirled around. Tired parents studied the departure board. Peter went to pick up our tickets. I stood and waited for the gate number to appear. I called Amy, my college roommate. Amy had been calling me every night since she started working the late shift. She was going to be visiting her in-laws.

'Hey.'

'Hey, what's up?' she said, sounding tired.

'I'm at Penn Station, and I don't want to go,' I said, sweating in my big coat.

'It will be fine.'

'They don't know we smoke. I'll have to sneak around like I'm fourteen again. The sister is a Jesus freak. The brother and the brother's girlfriend, Sue, who is hot and is studying to be a doctor ... a fucking doctor. How do I compete with that? What do I do? I'm fat, and I do nothing.'

'You're working on your thesis.'

'Amy, I'm not.'

'They don't know that.'

'Amy, I'm using.'

'When did that start?'

'I never stopped.' I had told her I stopped. 'But I stopped today. Today I'm clean.'

'Good,' she said. 'Are you anxious?'

'I need a Xanax, and we haven't even boarded the train.'

'Yeah, well, pause for a moment and feel bad for me. I'm in weirdo white trash world Upstate with Dennis.'

'Yeah, how's his mother?'

'Maya, this morning I woke up, and she was sitting on the couch dipping saltines in a jar of generic mayonnaise. Watching an infomercial like it was a real show.'

'That's disgusting,' I laughed.

'There was a pork chop on the counter. I mean, with no plate or napkin or anything.'

'Get out off the phone. The train is boarding,' Peter said, tickets in hand.

'I got to get on the train. I'll call you,' I said.

'Okay. Have fun.'

The train would have made a great target for a terrorist attack. It was packed.

'I don't think we'll be able to sit together,' I said as we slowly made our way through the car.

'Shouldn't we at least check the next car?'

'We could, but what's the point?' I said, eyeing the car for an empty seat by the window. There wasn't one. I collapsed in an aisle seat. Peter stood there like a wounded child. A woman in the next aisle stood up and offered him the window seat next to her.

I kept my eyes out the window.

I closed my eyes. If there was a bomb, it would be so fast. What would I feel? Probably heat and pain, and then nothing. It could happen any second. The train started bumping along. No such luck. Mom, in that big house in the suburbs slowly wasting away, always complaining of her failing body. The thought of a quick death didn't seem like the worst thing. Age is meaner than death.

There were trees and sky, and the city receded farther and farther behind us. Another world. It was hot. I wanted to take off my coat. I thought that ten more times before I actually took it off. I'd worn my denim skirt and a red blouse. At home in front of the mirror, sucking in my stomach, it had looked elegant, but as I sat there, my fat rolls pushing against the elastic of my skirt and falling over the top button, it felt awful. My stomach growled. The worst was to feel both fat and hungry.

Peter came over. 'Want to go to the dining car?'

'Yeah, okay.'

The only thing Suboxone didn't help with was the sweats. The back of my head and neck were wet.

The windows were huge, and the air felt easier to breathe. We sat in a booth.

'Can you buy me a bottle of water?' I asked him.

'I only have two singles.'

'Just use your card.'

'I don't know if they take cards.'

'For Chrissake, Peter, go and check. I'm dying of thirst.' He got up. Cheap bastard. Never wanted to spend a penny. He rolled his own cigarettes and refilled my old water bottles to take to work with him, even though he made good money. When we'd first met, he worked in the bookstore as a merchandiser and made next to nothing. 'I make everything pyramid shaped,' he'd said on our first date. What good was all that nagging to get a better paying job if he still refused to spend a dime? 'But we're making more money,' I would say. 'Yeah, well, we need to save it.' I'd asked a million times but never really understood what we were saving for. He came back with a brown box and a can of beer, a bottle of water, two packs of M&M's, and chips. He sat down in front of me. His eyes, as innocent and guilty as a child's, tried to gain my forgiveness.

'I had to spend at least ten dollars to use my card,' he explained.

'Oh, thanks,' I said. He was trying to be nice.

'Are you mad?'

'You were just being so awful this morning.' All morning, bustling around like a maniac, sighing and cursing to himself. Annoying the shit out of me.

'I'm sorry. I just get so anxious. Can we please just try to be nice to each other? I don't want to have a bad time.' As if I did? That was the implication, that I wanted everyone to be miserable. He popped open the Bud and took a long sip. *Great,* I thought, *just drink. Go be fucked-up in your world, and leave me here alone to deal with reality.*

Lily Tomlin once said, 'Reality is a crutch for people who can't cope with drugs.'

'Okay, well, don't act like a jerk,' I said.

'Can we please just watch *The Simpsons* on the laptop?'

He opened the laptop while I looked out the window, trying to decide whether or not to let him off the hook. My brain was tired. The sky looked so open outside of New York, not just above, but all around. A few brown trees, open fields. People were always saying how crowded the world was becoming, but outside of that window, there was so much space left.

Grace, Peter's sister, met us at the train station. She was wearing a flowered, matronly dress and, strangely, one white glove. She hugged us. I was pissed I couldn't sneak in a cigarette before she came.

It was colder. I zipped up my coat and buttoned it. They walked ahead, Peter carrying my two canvas bags and his one small tote.

Christ, I thought. *It's happening. We're really here.*

'What happened to your hand?' Peter asked Grace in the car.

'Oh, I burned it. I was frying zucchini in a pan and put in too much oil, and I tried pouring some of the oil out into a bowl, and it dripped down my hand.' She laughed the way girls laugh, like, 'I'm such an idiot, aw shucks.'

'That sucks,' I said. Peter shot me a look. 'Sucks' wasn't the right word. Should have gone with awful. 'How awful'; that would have been the right thing.

It was an unspoken rule that everyone dealt with Grace with kid gloves. Grace was the type of girl that had 'victim' written on her forehead. She was so trusting and so unsure of herself.

'So, what did you think of Sue?' Peter asked. His voice had changed already. A little bit more corny.

'Oh, she is *so* nice. Last night she helped with dinner, and she's so much fun, which is good for Jake. You know how serious he is.' Her face relaxed in a little smile.

Helped with dinner? Oh god, this Sue was worse than I thought. When I came to visit two Christmases ago, I hadn't helped with anything. I caught the flu on the train down and spent the entire four days of our visit shivering or sleeping in their clapboard house. Only one small TV in the enclosed porch that the whole family crowded around. Peter's mother bringing bowls of chicken broth, his father not knowing what to say, eyeing me.

'I thought you liked working at the bookstore,' his father had said when Peter told them about his new bartending job I had 'encouraged' him to get. Jesus, why did he have to implicate me in it? So now I was this girl who made their son work himself to death in some sinful place so he could buy more stuff for his fat wife to stare at.

At least it wasn't Christmas. On Christmas, Peter's mother, Sandy, sat down and asked if I knew the story of how Jesus was born. 'Like, in a barn,' I had said. And then she told the story with the wise men. It was long and didn't make a whole lot of sense. Their depressing tree and his mother wearing a reindeer sweater would break your heart. I got thermals. Peter got socks. They talked with unabashed glee about how cheap the gifts they got for one another were. It was like upside-down world. 'There was a bin marked 50 percent off,' Grace said as her father admired the gloves. 'Oh wow, and they're green,' someone said about their socks. You had to keep saying nice things. I wasn't very good at it. There was a detectable moment when I opened a present that my disappointment showed. The whole thing was so weird – to spend as little money as possible and to be as excited as little kids about receiving stuff that sucked. How was this fun? What was I going to do with these green paisley slippers made for a five-year-old? Without a word, I instantly put them on. Peter texted me; I hadn't said thank you, so I said, 'I forgot to say thank you. I love these slippers.' I couldn't pull it off. I should never have said anything.

I tried every year to teach them about gift giving by giving them actually nice things, but this seemed to embarrass them, like I didn't understand the cheapness rule. One time I gave them each an eight-dollar bacon-chocolate bar from Whole Foods in their stockings, and really nice bubble bath stuff for Sandy, perfume for Grace, an iPod speaker that looked like a panda for Jake, and for their father, an iPod shuffle. They eyed the bacon-chocolate bars and wouldn't even open them. I tried not to get involved when Peter bought his family gifts, but it was hard not to interject and pick out better things.

We pulled into the driveway. The sky looked naked without any buildings to cover it. The house was small and yellow. Before I could figure out a way to sneak off to smoke, Grace nodded at me to follow her through the side entrance.

Everything was way too bright and way too noisy. I thought of the sanctuary of Elizabeth's bedroom when she was strung out: darkness and a movie playing on a tiny laptop screen. Candles. Getting off dope was like coming back from the dead and like being reborn. The way to kick was to make the world as warm and womblike as possible. The birth experience of the bustling scene at Peter's parent's house was jarring and raw. Everything hit too hard, and emotions came out of nowhere. Their sad little house they were so proud of. How they had worked hard and done their best. How they loved their children. No matter where you went on Earth, there were parents who loved their kids and wanted to know everything they did and laughed at their jokes.

Behind me, Peter was carrying all of our bags like a Sherpa. Their skinny, tired son carrying all the bags while I walked in empty handed.

'Oh, it's so good to see you,' Peter's mother said as she embraced me. His father asked if Peter needed help. Peter shook his head. 'Where are we sleeping?' he asked.

'In Jake's old room,' his father said. Peter walked to the back of the house, leaving me there with all of them. Sue walked in, thin-boned, wearing blue jeans and a tight black sweater, her hair in a ponytail. We shook hands. 'You look so cold,' she said. Her body was perfect. Her smile showed ultrawhite teeth. She was a ray of sunshine. I was doom and gloom and could hardly muster a smile. I wanted her to like me. I hated her instantly.

'Yeah, I'm kind of cold.' I was still wearing my coat. I kept waiting for the warmth to hit me after I came in, but there was no heat.

'Oh, sorry about that,' Sandy said.

You couldn't say, 'Please turn on the heat because I can't stop shivering in your freezing shitty house.' You couldn't say, 'I'm just going to go to a bedroom because I'd rather read than talk to any of you.' You couldn't say, 'This is my first day off dope, and all of this is overwhelming.' You couldn't say, 'Let's cut the bullshit. You don't give a shit where I'm from, just like I have no interest in any of the questions I will force myself to ask so I don't appear rude. So I'll just shut myself in your freezing porch and watch your shitty television until it's time to go, and you can ignore me and hang out with your kid.'

'No, it's fine,' I smiled.

Sue opened the oven door and looked in.

'Are you making something?' I asked.

'Yeah, a pie,' she said. A fucking pie?

'Like, from scratch?' I asked, trying not to look down her top at her tits. She was wearing a hot pink bra.

'Yeah, me and Jake found the recipe last night, so this morning we all went to the market, and I bought the ingredients.'

'Why are you still wearing your coat?' Peter, coatless, asked. *How can any of them stand it*, I wondered.

'She's cold. Maybe I can ask your father to start the fire.'

Jake wrapped his arms around Sue and said, 'Maybe just turn the heat on.' Why did they have to be touching? It felt obscene somehow, like they were so obsessed with each other they had to always be touching. I wanted to be touched. I was pretty sure I would puke if anyone touched me.

'What's going on?' Sue asked.

'Maya's cold, so we were thinking of telling your father to put the heat on,' Sandy said.

'Or we could put the fire on?' Grace replied.

'No, I'm … it's okay, I don't mind …' But she was already walking away, calling, 'Rick,' and then I heard my name. I should have just taken off my coat.

'Yeah, but the fire will take longer to warm the house, and we can't have her sit there alone in front of the fire,' Sandy said.

Peter's father came down. 'What's up?'

'We were talking about putting the heat on.'

'The heat?' He wiped his forehead.

'Maya's cold,' Sandy said.

'I can put the fire on …'

I wanted to literally vanish into thin air.

'We haven't met, I'm Peter,' Peter said to Sue.

'Hey, Jake's told me so much about you.' Sue put on Sandy's apron. It had cherries all over it. I walked past Peter to Jake's old bedroom and shut the door. I imagined my entire bag filled with heroin. Then all of this would have been very easy. Why did I even try to be clean? *All my effort should have gone toward staying high all the time,* I thought. I could smile and talk and be charming when I was high. I wasn't self-conscious and weird. If not for me, then for the world. I started sweating. What could I do now? Tell them not to put the heat on and go through that whole hundred-year-long conversation. Sue and her amazing pie and her skinny waist and her smile – I wondered what it was like to be inside her head. She probably had her own insecurities. I needed a cigarette. I checked the time: five o'clock. *Two hours of awkward conversations, and then just stuff your face and sit around the dining table for a while, and then off to bed.* They went to sleep early, ten-ish. Just five hours. I fished out my cigarettes and my cell phone from my canvas bag.

I wanted a bag of dope so fucking bad. If I was sick, I could convince them to take me to the train, and then I'd go back home and get a bag. A rush of excitement filled me at the thought. It was okay, I would get high again. This was not for forever. This was like a job. A bad shift at a bad job.

After being numb for so long on dope, when I was finally faced with reality, I couldn't handle the emotions. Not just the bad ones. The in between ones too, like envious that Peter got along with his family, grateful these people were being nice to me and were willing to love me just for being there, and nostalgic when they played that Dylan song Peter sang on our first date. They wanted to like me, and all it did was make me feel lonely and insecure. I wiped the tears away and told myself to get it together. I was a grown-up and needed to act like one.

Back in the kitchen, Peter's mother stood in front of a pot of some kind of meat, Sue and Peter chatted it up, and Rick held a plate of the cheeses Peter and I had bought yesterday at Whole Foods. That was the difference; Peter and I bought expensive cheese from Whole Foods while Sue baked a pie from scratch. That Sandy's apron looked so cute on her was also troubling.

No one noticed me open the window. I was sweating through my clothes. I smelled like something that had died in the trash. At least if it was cold, I wouldn't smell as bad.

'I should really go and call my mom,' I said to no one in particular, holding my phone as if they needed a visual aid. I turned and walked out, trying not to look at Peter's face.

'Can you just not smoke for two fucking days,' he had said when I asked if I had to keep up this charade that we didn't smoke.

I opened the door. Couldn't stand right there, so I turned the corner and then realised there was a window, and they would see me from the dining room. I walked back toward Jake's old room and fished out a cigarette and then hit 'mom' on my phone.

She picked up right away.

'Hey,' she said weakly.

'Hi.'

'Where are you?'

'We just got here.'

'How is it?'

'I don't know, Mom, I feel so out of place.' The cigarette tasted so good. My body started to feel right as the nicotine hit me, but then I felt a little woozy from not smoking all day. I crouched down.

'What do you mean?'

'They're just so nice.'

'So?'

'It's weird. I don't know what to say.'

'Raj wants to talk to you,' and before I could protest, my brother was on the phone.

'What's going on?'

'Oh, Raj, it's like, they're like a normal family,' I said as I lit a new cigarette from the one I just smoked.

'You're lucky, I bet the food is good. Mom couldn't cook, so we're having leftover lasagna and watching *Colombo*.'

'Yeah, it seems like there's a lot of ...' and then I heard Mom in the background, 'Tell her not to eat too much, she's already gained so much weight.' Why did she always have to be awful?

'Mom says not to eat too much.'

'I heard.' I heard my mom again, 'Potatoes, tell her,' and then she got back on the phone. 'Don't eat the potatoes, you know, carbs. Just eat some turkey and the vegetables.' You would have thought someone with her kind of medical problems would realise how silly something like counting calories was, but somehow after she got sick she'd become even worse, like she was clinging to these little things as the last fringes of her mom-hood or personhood. The whole thing was so depressing.

'Yeah, okay.'

'Where are you?' Raj again.

'I'm out smoking a cigarette.' I put it out on the cold ground and stuck the butt back into the pack.

'You should probably go back in there.'

'Yeah, okay. Bye.'

He said goodbye. It could have been worse. I could have been with them. A small leafless tree stood in front of me. Another house, blue against the grey sky. Peter hated winter. He said it was like death all around. But there was something beautiful about this naked tree in the wind.

Samuel Beckett said, 'Nothing is more real than nothing.'

I walked back into the house and took off my coat. I was covered in sweat, and the house was so hot it made it hard to breathe. I opened a window. I made my way to the plate of cheese we brought, and the crackers. Whenever I saw food, I felt compelled to eat it, even if I wasn't hungry. Jake came in. I nodded, but he went in for a hug.

'Hey,' he said, looking at me, smiling. Jake could be so handsome it was almost startling. There wasn't even any sexual tension between us because it didn't feel like we were the same species. It was kind of a relief to hang out with people where you didn't have to think about if you wanted to fuck them or if they wanted to fuck you.

'So, how's it going?' I asked, stuffing my mouth. I started shivering again. Why did I have to wear the thinnest blouse in my closet?

'You're still cold?' he asked with genuine concern. 'Someone opened the window,' he said, and then went over and closed it. 'Who would do that?'

That was when I should've confessed, but I didn't. I couldn't seem to get warm. I put my coat back on, and my scarf. I was shaking. My face hurt. My sinuses were congested. One day someone would pick up my skull and say, 'This human has the worst sinuses I've ever seen. It must have been horrible to live like that.' Sweat poured out of my pits. I could smell the dopesick stench. A kind of rotting.

'I'm so glad you finally met Sue.'

'Yeah,' I said. We sat there and smiled. Grace walked in. I hoped she couldn't smell me.

'You're still cold?' I realised I was standing with my arms around me, crouched over. I stood upright.

'No, no, I'm fine.'

'Did you open the window?' Jake asked her.

The front door opened. I braced myself to withstand a gust

of wind. A middle-aged man wearing a snowflake sweater came in beside a short-haired woman in high-waisted light blue jeans.

'Jake!' The man slipped his arm around Jake.

'Hi, I'm Marcie,' the woman said. Aunt Marcie, Peter had mentioned her. The aunt who made that ratatouille Peter raved about.

'Hi, I'm Maya, Peter's wife.'

'Well, it's so good to meet you.' We smiled. It had been Peter's idea to go off to Vegas and get married. I thought it would be like running away, but when I met his relatives, it felt like I was this mysterious woman they were all wondering about.

'Darren,' the man introduced himself, smiling, his face friendly. 'Wow,' he said, 'It is so nice to finally meet you.' I smiled back. 'So, huh, it must be what, two years since the two of you got married?'

'No, about four.'

'Didn't want to deal with the fuss of a big wedding, I guess?' he said, taking his gloves off and putting them on the kitchen table. The table had a plastic tablecloth on it.

'I guess that was part of it, but it was more like we thought it would be fun, you know?'

'Right, right,' he said, smiling, nodding, as if fun were something he had a working understanding of. Marcie stood and observed us.

It felt like Darren was the talk show host; me, the guest; and Marcie, our audience.

'We got married by Elvis,' I said. It was what I said every time I mentioned the wedding.

'Huh! How fun! I would love to see pictures,' he said, still smiling. I believed him. He really would have loved to see pictures.

'Oh, I don't have any. We didn't think to take any.'

'Yeah …'

'We were pretty loaded,' I said. A moment passed. 'I'm kidding,' I added.

Darren burst into laughter; Marcie, a cautious smile.

'Yeah, you guys just met that night, right?' Darren said, adding to the joke.

'Actually, we met there at the chapel.'

Darren laughed harder.

Peter and his father came in. Nervous, I smeared goat cheese on another cracker and stuffed it in my mouth. I wanted to throw up, and I was sweating again.

'So, what do you say, should I open a bottle of wine?' Rick said to Darren.

'Can I see it?' Peter said. I loved how Peter acted as if knowing wine was an actual hobby of his, when it was just like what watching porn was for a sex addict. The culture of wine, learning obscure cocktails, having just a beer. He was a fucking alcoholic.

'I say, sounds like a great idea,' Darren said. Peter walked over and put his arm around me, which made me uncomfortable. I hated the way he was always touching me. My stomach cramped. I was going to have the runs.

There was only one fucking bathroom, and someone was in there, taking forever. You couldn't say, 'I seriously will shit myself if you don't stop fucking touching me.'

On the toilet, I doubled over in pain. I wanted to fucking die. When I stood up, my vision darkened. I sat back down on the toilet lid. I closed my eyes. Did I need to puke or shit? Did I need more Suboxone, or had I taken too much? I stood up. Shit on the floor and puke in the toilet, or puke on the floor and shit in the toilet? I lay down on the cool tiles with my eyes closed. Get it together. Grow up. Get it together. Darkness. Self-loathing. Regret. I was an addict. I wasn't an addict; I was just in a fucked-up situation. I was going to end up homeless. Everything would be fine. I needed to use a lifeline. I needed to ask the studio audience. I needed to phone a friend.

I let myself cry for a minute.

Eventually you had to say to yourself, 'Get over yourself.'

Peter's father took Darren down the hall somewhere. Sue reappeared, humming, in her apron, ready to take out her pie. Jake was putting something in a pan. 'Did you make something?' I asked him.

'Yeah, just an apple crisp.'

'Yeah, we bought some apples this morning, and we browned them with sugar,' Sue added.

'Huh,' I said, deadpan. It had been only two hours, and already I was exhausted by faking enthusiasm.

Peter's mom chopped something and Peter left again. I was just standing there, in the kitchen. There was an empty chair at the dining table so I sat down, but then it was like I was sitting there while everyone else was doing something. I stood back up. 'Do you need help?' I asked. No one heard me. So. Huh. I sat back down.

The wine. Find the wine.

I found a glass. 'Do you want something to drink?' Sandy asked.

'Where is the wine?'

'Oh,' she said, and then she came closer, 'about the wine. Grace is, well, you remember, over Christmas. She's touchy about having wine in the house, you know. She has her beliefs. So we compromised; we're keeping the wine in the other room.' She smiled, apologetically.

Grace went to a religious college and lived in a 'sober dorm.' If she was lame as a college student, how lame could she possibly get as an adult? Or would the lameness build up and then she would reach forty and become addicted to coke and rediscover God? Or would she maintain her lameness until she died? Or maybe she had a different measurement for lameness, and in her own world, like, eating ice cream past midnight and talking all night was her being wild. Was lameness subjective? Was it something we grew out of or something we eventually had to experience?

A boy. She would meet the wrong boy, and then anything could happen. It was always like that: girl is fine, meets boy, falls in love, ruins life, boy leaves, girl straightens life out, dusts

Bible, puts on lame dress, and goes back to church. At least then she would have something to repent for, experiences to regret. I wished I could have given her some of mine. I wished I were someone no one ever had to worry about. I should have been with my mother who was dying of MS. I should have saved money and bought her nice presents. A knot in my stomach. I wanted to hug my mom. I felt the future me looking back at the selfish me, who spent all her time avoiding her sick mother, staying high, and being a huge disappointment.

Last Christmas Grace and Rick got into a big fight with Peter about having alcohol in the house. They compromised and kept the alcohol away from Grace. They must have made the same arrangement. 'Just don't cross the line into the dining room,' Sandy said into my ear as she poured my glass. I nodded, like this was all very reasonable.

Wasn't part of Jesus's whole thing turning water into wine?

Two Xanaxes and two glasses of wine later, I felt amazing. Xanax was like a shortcut out of the woods of addiction and into the clearing of sobriety. Fucking Xanax. I could do this every month or so. Get clean, let my dope tolerance drop so I wouldn't need to use as much to get high, save money, stay clean for long stretches – but still have dope when I needed it. I could use until Peter and I had babies, and then slide right back into society, blend into Facebook with baby pictures, my hair in a baseball cap, complain about how tired I was in my status updates. Life would take over, and like a mountain climber,

I would keep going. A stupid, idiotic mountain climber moving very slowly up a big, dumb mountain, weighed down by a bag of shit, finding one foothold at a time, just to turn around and do it all over again backwards. All this until you wake up one day, and you are old. Your kid has taken over, and you become part of the shit they have to carry with them. Just like my mother, haunting me. If only she was kind enough to become a memory. Memories didn't call. Memories didn't nag. Memories stayed golden and young, and you kept the ones you wanted. Memories didn't have lesions on their brains and chairs in their showers. She used to be young and pretty. Did she know, when she opened the oven to check on dinner, that taking care of kids was how she was wasting the best years of her life? That was what I was aspiring to do, but at least I knew it. At least I experienced college and watched enough television with female leads to know exactly what I would regret. She wasn't stupid. Having a family was a popular way to waste your life, so maybe it wasn't the worst way. You had to do something or do nothing. She knew she would have finite time to be in her physical prime, so why did I feel bad? Why did I have to be implicated? Why did I feel guilty that she had wasted it on me? She lived the life she wanted. It was her choice not to finish school, not to have a career, to marry an old man she didn't love. She had her eyes wide open.

All the pain went back to my mother. Freud didn't seem that deep. It was natural to contemplate the very beginning and the first person you ever met, whose job was to keep you alive when everything was brand-new, and you were perfect with all kinds of perfect futures. I popped another Xanax. Things were going to be absolutely fine.

Peter's father, at the head of the table, said, 'Okay, I guess we'll start.' I nodded, but something was wrong because I was the only one still standing up. Then I realised Darren had my hand, and I looked around. *Oh, right, the praying.*

'Thank you, Lord, for the food we are about to receive ...'

It was just like the movies! 'And for the animals who gave their lives for us to have this meal and ...' This struck me as hysterical. The animals? Like they agreed to be sacrificed? Then that feeling hit me, the one where you knew you weren't supposed to laugh, so all you wanted to do was laugh. I bit down on my lip, hard.

After the prayer, I shot straight up to the buffet and filled my plate with green beans and a heap of mashed potatoes, and put the plate down to slice some meat. 'Maya, don't forget about the onions, they're over there,' Peter's father pointed across the room.

'Did you make them?' I asked.

'I grew 'em,' he smiled.

I couldn't tell if he was being serious. 'Wow, that's, um, I didn't know you could do that,' I said, meaning growing food when the ground was so cold, but it sounded like I didn't know anyone could grow anything.

'So, Sue, how's medical school going? Tackling cadavers?'

Darren asked. I burst into laughter. Everyone looked at me.

'No, I'm sorry, I just didn't know it was a phrase, 'tackling cadavers.'' There was a general laugh. Darren cracked up, putting his hand on my shoulder like we were old friends. Was that mean to say? Was I making fun of him?

When my food was gone, I got more.

Later I crouched in front of the toilet and put my fingers down my throat and dry-heaved and did it again and again and finally it all came up. I sat on the floor, exhausted. Then I ate vanilla ice cream because when you threw it up it didn't burn. I wasn't just throwing up because of the calories; I was trying to take care of the future me that was going to wake up dope sick with a stomach full of food. I stared at the mirror. My eyes were watery, and my face flushed. The Xanax had faded. I would have to keep taking more, and then it would knock me out. I couldn't go on like this. I would sleep forever, be high forever, and be broke forever.

After dinner I thought about helping clear the table, but Sue and Grace beat me to it.

Peter's mother handed out pens and sheets of paper. 'I don't know if the boys told you,' she said to me and Sue, 'but we have this tradition of writing down what we're thankful for, and then we put it in that vase,' she pointed to a shiny blue vase. 'Then we go around the table and everyone takes one out and reads it, and everyone guesses who wrote what. It's just this silly tradition …'

As she walked away, I noticed she was kind of waddling.

Sue looked thoughtfully at her paper. Close up she had bad skin, with makeup caked over the blemishes. Sometimes the thing that solved the problem was the bigger problem.

'I'm thankful I have this glass of alcohol,' I whispered to Sue. She giggled.

'I'm thankful for having locked in a low interest rate,' I said loud enough for Darren to hear. He snorted. I was making fun of this family tradition. I had never realised how jokes were always a little mean. That was why these people never joked around. My mother and me and Raj were always laughing, when we weren't screaming at each other.

'I am thankful I have a cozy apartment to come home to every night.'

'Peter!' I yelled. No one else said anything. I guess we were not supposed to literally shout.

Peter nodded, 'Yup.'

Sue dug one out. 'I am thankful for having a mother who taught us the value of sacrifice.'

No one said anything. Finally Sandy said, 'Marcie.' Marcie nodded. So Marcie was Peter's mother's sister. They didn't really look alike. Marcie was as skinny as a jackrabbit, with a dyke haircut and a warm smile. Sandy's face was as long as Sunday, and her body was wide and heavy, like mine would be if I ever had kids and got to sixty.

'I am thankful to Jesus,' some number or chapter of the Bible I didn't really hear, 'and have been thinking and praying on the idea of judgment and hoping the Lord will guide me to a state of mind where I will not cast judgment on anyone.' I pointed to Rick. 'That was you, huh?' He nodded. I told myself I should quit guessing and give other people a chance.

I wished I could stop talking. I couldn't stop talking. I had nothing to say.

'I am thankful for not living in poverty, being in pain, or having too little or too much, but most the time feeling all right, and even good, full of good food and wine, and good company like tonight.' There was a general mmm and aw.

'A writer wrote that,' Darren said, and everyone nodded. 'Maya, was that you?'

I nodded. When in doubt just ramble a little, Kerouac style.

Peter's mother gave me an approving nod. 'Very nice,' she said.

It was Peter's turn. 'I am thankful for friends, new and old,' he read. He refilled his wine glass. He was obviously wasted.

Grace guessed, 'Sue?'

Sue nodded. Friends new and old. Hallmark bullshit.

It was my turn. I took one out. 'I am thankful to the Lord for keeping me safe and well during my travels.' Grace had just come back from Italy.

I had completely lost interest. I mentally replayed how impressed everyone had been with what I wrote.

'After dinner the men sat on the living room floor and sang songs while the women cleaned up the kitchen,' I told my therapist a week later, and then buried my head into a pillow.

'Where were you?'

'I lingered in the kitchen, but every time I grabbed a pot and took it to the counter there was no space for it, so Sandy had to move this huge, heavy blender, like, just so I could put down the mashed potatoes. I was making things more difficult for her. I started doing the dishes, but she said, 'Don't worry about it. There's a dishwasher.' Sue was loading the dishwasher and made me feel dumb for not thinking of it. I am not good that way. I don't know how she seamlessly blends in and knows where everything goes. Some people can just get into the rhythm of things, but I never know how. But then I feel bad that I'm not helping, like I'm being rude. The truth is I don't really want to help. I just don't want to look like an asshole, and it's not fair, because men aren't expected to do this stuff, like there's this rule if you have a vagina you are programmed to wash dishes or sweep the floor or whatever. Also, you know when people say, 'It's okay, I'll do it,' are you supposed to do it anyway or take their word for it? Because I always take their word for it. Some people really don't want you to be all up in their shit, so how are you supposed to know?'

'Were you this anxious the whole time?'

'No, once I just gave up on trying to help, I went and sat on the living room floor and listened to music and everyone was so happy. It was weird. I didn't know people did stuff like that in real life. It made me so uncomfortable.' I talked with my hand over my face.

'What about it was uncomfortable?'

'I am jealous he grew up in this warm, loving environment where people cared about things, like writing, and people just liked each other. Whenever my family got together for the holidays, all the kids just sat in front of the TV while our parents talked about money, houses, the prices of this or that, real estate. It was awful. No one in my family even knows I can write, but I write a few lines on a piece of paper and Peter's family is impressed.'

'Every family has their problems. They were probably on their best behavior for the holidays,' she said.

'No, I mean, maybe, but at least they could fake that well. I felt it. It was nice; they actually listened to each other. At first it made me anxious and crazy, but once I got drunk it was really nice.'

'What about a family being warm and polite makes you anxious when you're sober?'

'I always have this feeling I'm going to fuck it up somehow. Like I'm walking on eggshells, and then it's this impulse control thing. I keep thinking, What if I just said 'Fuck' really loud? What would happen?'

The morning after Thanksgiving I woke up shivering. I had to pee. I lay there until I was in physical pain. I poked Peter in the face.

'Whhhat?' he yawned, after the third or fourth poke.

'I'm freezing.'

'So?'

'Fix it,' I said.

'Didn't you bring a sweater or something?' He rolled over to face the wall. He was always rolling over and facing the wall. It was no use. There was no way I could fall asleep again. The only way I had fallen asleep in the first place was all the Xanax and the wine. Then the nausea hit. It was my second day of being clean. I made myself get out from under the covers and find the Suboxone in my purse. I put it under my tongue and then took two Xanaxes. Suboxone dissolving underneath the tongue is unpleasant. It made me gag. I was covered in sweat and shivering. I went back to bed till the Xanax kicked in. I took a shit in the bathroom. Popped two more Xanaxes. You can't be too frugal with the Xanax the first few days. Soon the Suboxone would kick in and give me a nice buzz and some energy. I couldn't imagine doing this without any meds. I would be naked in corner, bawling and vomiting, my shit-covered drawers on the floor, and no one on Earth would sit in that room without praying I would fall asleep for a while. Peter would leave me to hang out with his family or to work or whatever. He wouldn't take a wet rag and wipe my face. He wouldn't try to feed me a spoonful of broth. He would tell me to take a shower. He would lay out clean clothes. He would gasp with relief as soon as he walked out the door and could think whatever he wanted. Bad things. And because marriage is really a war, he would have new weapons to use against me: 'Oh, the junkie says I'm an alcoholic.' I found my phone and put my smokes in my coat. After I took a piss, I went to the fridge. I had already decided I wasn't going to eat today, but I wanted to look at the food like a weirdo.

Peter's mother and father came into the kitchen. 'Where'd you guys go?' I asked, shutting the fridge. I was slurring a little and having a hard time standing. *Don't lean on the fridge. Don't furrow your brows like every word they say takes all your concentration to understand.* I put my face back in the fridge. Was it rude to dig around someone's fridge? They said to make myself at home, but did they mean it? Why couldn't people just say what they meant?

'I had some blood drawn for my surgery next week,' Sandy said.

'What surgery?'

Rick smelled the milk.

'Hip surgery,' she said. That's why she waddled.

'Are you in pain?'

'Well, it's gotten worse, but once they replace the hip, it should be fine,' she said, washing a dish. If it had been my mother, no one would have heard the end of it. 'Here I am with a broken hip, but don't mind me. I'll just end up dying here, washing your dishes.'

'I'll be right back,' I said, not bothering to show them the phone. I would be making idiots of us all if I kept pretending I wasn't going out to smoke. I must have reeked.

The day was bright, and the air was crisp and clean. The Suboxone must have started to kick in because I felt a surge of euphoria. I knew I was going to have a horrible time in the bathroom, but right then I felt pretty awesome. A little too awesome. Giddy. Excited. Kind of manic. I walked over to the shed and lit a cigarette. Then I heard a car door slam. Fuck. I put out the cigarette on the ground.

Jake, Sue and Peter were milling around the kitchen in their boots and coats. I embraced Peter and kissed him. 'Why is everyone dressed? Where are we going?'

'Rake leaves,' he said.

'Are there enough rakes?' I asked, praying to an imaginary god there were not.

'Yeah.'

We walked outside. Leaning against the shed were four rakes. I ran back into the house and grabbed my iPod. *Some Young Buck, some Lil Wayne, some JaySZ should keep me pumped.*

Everyone spread to opposite corners. I picked up a red rake and walked to the far left of the yard. Jay-Z, in my ears, 'Ain't no love, in the heart of the city.' The sun was out and warmed my face. I had boundless energy. I formed the leaves into a pile like connecting the dots, forming the smaller piles into one large pile. When I had most of my corner of the yard raked, I yelled for Peter. He looked up at me and shook his head.

'Maya, that's where the leaves are going to be dumped.'

'What? I don't get it,' I told him.

'Where you're raking, that's where the leaves are going to go. We are going to take all the leaves in this yard,' he waved his hand, signifying the rest of the yard, 'and put them in this corner,' he said, pointing at the ground I'd just cleared.

'Why wouldn't we throw the leaves away?'

99

'We gather them all in that corner,' he repeated, sounding like a little kid. I cracked up. I couldn't stop laughing. Peter smiled, but I could tell he was trying to figure out if I was high or crazy.

I looked over and saw Sue laughing with a wheelbarrow full of leaves, with her cute little hat, her pink pj's tucked into a pair of cowboy boots. Where did she even get a wheelbarrow? Jake helped Sue, both of them laughing, like in a montage at the beginning of a cheesy sitcom, rushing across the yard. I watched them dump the big mass of wet leaves into the corner I had worked so hard to clear.

Peter's father came out with a tarp. We heaped the leaves onto the tarp, and then Peter, his father, and Jake lifted the tarp from the sides and dumped the leaves in the corner. What the fuck was the point of this? Why weren't we throwing them away? I wanted to ask, but then I didn't really care either. We spent all morning putting a bunch of leaves into a corner of a yard where they were going to get spread all over the place again. Whatever. Doing stuff was dumb.

Sue said, 'They said it was going to rain, but it looks clear.' She gave me a gracious smile.

'So, kids,' Peter's dad said, 'I want you to know when the economy gets bad or if you ever need to, you're all welcome to come back and live here. We can grow our own food, see,' he pointed to some ground, 'that's where I grow vegetables ... and you know, we could just all live here.'

My eyes got wet. I wanted to burst into tears imagining how he must have thought about this and was naive and sweet enough to think of all of us living here like this forever. Ignoring, of course, the weird paranoia about society crumbling.

'Dad, I don't think it's going to get that bad,' Jake said, looking slightly pained. And everyone kind of laughed, but I didn't, because a part of me *did* want to move there and grow our own food and get a dog and have dinner at the table every night and sit Indian-style on the floor and listen to them sing songs.

We headed into the house. I sat down at the kitchen table while Peter's mother scrambled eggs. I was ready to stuff my face again. Peter nudged my arm, and I went to the enclosed porch with him. We sat on the couch.

'I love you,' he said in my ear.

'Yeah, I love you too.'

'What's wrong?'

'I don't know … wasn't really into raking leaves.' There was a pause and then I said, 'Whatever, it was fine. I'm tired.' I said it as a way of getting out of the whole thing.

'You didn't have to.'

All of the sudden he looked good to me. So clean. So wholesome, with his big smile and flannel and dark jeans. The was fire going, and for the first time since I'd gotten there, I actually felt warm. I liked it there. 'What do you want to do?' he asked me, putting his arm around my shoulders. He smelled good.

'I want to check out some thrift stores,' I said.

'I'll ask Grace and Mom if they know any.' He smiled and walked back toward the kitchen. I leaned my head back against the cold boarded-over window. Sometimes I felt this horrible ache, like I already knew whatever was happening would become a memory I would think of and cry about after Peter left me. A premature nostalgia, like when you took a picture and imagined what it was going to be like one day to look at it and remember how happy you had been. A part of me was always mourning how painful it would feel after the happiness wore off. So I was never really happy, like, ever.

We all got in the car to drive to Burlington. Jake drove. Sue sat in the passenger seat playing with the radio, and Peter and I were in the backseat with Grace. My head on his shoulder.

'Are you excited about the thrift shop?' he whispered into my ear, in the same tone he used when we were fucking and he'd say, 'Yeah, you like that big cock deep inside your pussy?'

'Yeah, I can't wait.' I wanted to somehow convey how good I felt about him, but I didn't know how. If I took him aside and tried to express something deep, he would think I was trying to start some heavy fight. You couldn't say to a man, 'I really need to talk to you.' No man on Earth has ever wanted to talk.

The consignment store was in a little crappy house. Peter bought two shirts that I picked out for him for two dollars each. It was the best situation for us: I got whatever I wanted, and he got to pay for everything without that pained look on his face. I found salt and pepper shakers that looked like cheeseburgers and a small blue suitcase with white stitching. Sue and Jake bought a similar suitcase but more expensive, in better condition. We joked over how we should go on a trip together with our matching suitcases. Grace tried on jackets, but she obviously did not get the whole thrift store thing. How you were supposed to find things that were either practical or totally silly, not 'nice' things for a job interview. She tried on a worn green blazer from the Gap. Her fat strained the buttons as she stared into the mirror, and my heart broke for her. I guessed food was the only thing left once you took all the sinful stuff that made people feel good off the list. It hurt to see a hopeful look in her face, like, 'Well, this isn't bad at all, hmm.' But she looked terrible. Her greasy ponytail, the hair frizzing out by her ears, her bad skin. I wondered if she had ever seen a penis. If she ever touched herself. She must have had urges. Maybe she did and then felt really bad or cut herself. Maybe she was in love with Jesus. Or she was in love with her father. It was weird how she always deferred to him. In some families, the daughter and the father are the couple in a nonsexual but still creepy way.

'That looks nice,' I said.

'Yeah, it's only four dollars,' she said, still looking in the mirror. Her smile brightened.

After the thrift store, we went bowling.

'Did you see the Dunkin' Donuts when we drove in?' Sue said, as we waited for our shoes.

'Do you want donuts? I'll go get them,' I said. It was my ticket out of this group. My chance to stop smiling for a second.

I went outside and lit a cigarette. It was me and the grey sky. The nicotine hit me in a rush, a strange mixture of sadness and exhilaration. I steadied myself. I took out my phone and saw Amy had called. I called her back.

'Hey,' I said.

'They're so weird,' she whispered.

'Why are you whispering?

'I'm hiding in the bathroom.'

'Why?

'I'm never going to get rid of him.' Her voice quivered.

'Are you crying?'

'How am I ever going to break up with him? He would end up here if I threw him out. I've only been here for, like, two days or whatever, and I want to kill myself. His mother will not leave me alone. I went to the office to go on the internet, and she came with me and worked out on the bike, and then I went downstairs, and she came with me. I don't think she works. And his brother and his wife live with her, but they only have one car. How did I end up with this life that doesn't look like anything I wanted?'

'Just leave him already. It isn't your problem what happens to him. You didn't give birth to him, you know,' I said, frustrated. How many times had I said those words to her?

'Sometimes I just think, you know, I'm thirty-one, and if I want to have a kid, I've got to get going. Did you know that after thirty-five the rate of Down syndrome goes up?'

'Yeah, I've heard that.' This was actually the third time I'd heard that statistic in the past month. There was always this ticking clock, ruining everything little by little the longer you lived.

The Dunkin' Donuts was packed. There was nowhere else to go in town. Two old men came in behind me. The line wasn't moving. There was an image of an egg croissant with bacon. My mouth watered. They had hash browns now? I wanted it all. I wondered if there was a way to buy an egg sandwich, hash browns, and three Boston creams and scarf them all down without being suspiciously absent for too long. Then I could go puke it up. I was doing this more and more, sneaking food and then puking it up. I wasn't good at it yet, but it was awesome to stuff yourself and then have an empty stomach. One time last week I scarfed down five Hostess cupcakes before I came home and was caught when Peter asked innocently, 'Is that chocolate on your teeth?' It was exactly like when he found a bag of dope in my pockets.

The bathroom: Keeping America's secrets for decades. Snorting. Puking. Crying. Leaving weepy messages on Ogden's voicemail.

Whenever I talked to Ogden it was anticlimactic. To have all these feelings of wanting and longing, a hole in my heart and none of it translating into the dull words passing through my lips, 'I miss you,' or 'I think about you,' or 'I wish you were here.' They came out of my mouth and disappeared but the hole was still there.

'Hi, I'd like an egg sandwich with bacon, and hash browns and a dozen donuts,' I said. I turned just as Peter came in.

'What is taking so long?' he asked, annoyed. I ignored him and told the woman what donuts I wanted. Eyeing the overly large bag and the box of donuts the woman handed to me, he said, 'How many things did you order?'

I looked behind me. The place was completely empty except for two people. 'It was packed. It had nothing to do with how much stuff I ordered,' I huffed at him.

'Are you getting a dozen donuts?'

'Yeah, for everyone.'

'I'm sorry, honey.' He put his arm around me. 'I just didn't know what was taking so long.'

'I'm sorry I'm fat,' I said.

'Stop it, you know how annoying that is. I like you just the way you are,' he said, patting my fat butt.

We walked back to the bowling alley.

I sucked at bowling. Sue beat me, Jake beat Peter, and Grace couldn't play because of her burnt hand. I wondered if Jake fell asleep in front of the TV all the time like Peter. If he lay around in sweat shorts and old T-shirts on the couch, playing with his balls and generally being a disgusting man. Sometimes Peter itched his balls and smelled his hand afterwards. Was this something he had always done, and just now something he felt comfortable doing around me? Did he think I didn't notice, or did he not care? Why did balls itch so goddamn much?

After bowling we drove into Burlington and walked around. We found another thrift store and went in. Sue and I looked through the women's section together.

Peter found a leather jacket, like MacGyver's. It was terrible, the colour of mud or diarrhea, with some rips, and the waist was too short and puffy. The type of thing someone's dad would wear.

'Isn't it great?' Peter asked, smiling, so excited.

'I hate it.'

'What?' He looked like I had stabbed him. 'What do you hate about it?'

'I'm sure there's one that's better. Let me look.'

'No,' he said sternly, 'I looked through them all and this is the one I like the best.'

'It's just so bad. The colour, the fit.'

'It's only twenty dollars.'

'It's worth less.'

'Why are you being a bitch?' he said, walking away.

Mallard ducks. Peter had a tapestry of mallard ducks on his wall in his room in Queens. The ducks weren't cartoony. They weren't whimsical ducks going in every direction. They were serious ducks in serious colours, blank-eyed in straight rows like little communists. His dead grandmother had made it. Before I said something like, 'Can't you love her without displaying this awful thing on my wall?' I realised it meant a lot to him. He was like someone on *Hoarders* who thought the thing had to do with the person. There was also a frightful portrait of Winston Churchill his grandmother painted. I didn't say anything as Peter, without a second thought, put the mallard ducks up in the bedroom and the Winston Churchill in the center of the living room wall. I would forever be reading a book and look up to find this awful, fat, uniformed man in front of me.

The worst part about the ducks and Winston Churchill was they made me hate myself. Why did I care? If it made Peter happy, why wasn't that more important than my apartment? I had slowly but progressively filled my apartment with perfect things. That was why I spent forever finding the exact right fridge, stainless steel and tall, but thin, so it wouldn't go past the doorway of the narrow kitchen. The dish drainer was Swedish and costed seventy dollars. Instead of getting a regular toilet brush, I got something called a toilet wand with disposable toilet scrubbers. I spent a whole paycheck on one thing. I wanted my little corner of the world to be an uncluttered, peaceful masterpiece. And then Peter came in with his mallard ducks and his Winston Churchill and his collection of coloured bottles he put on every fucking surface. What was it with men and bottles? But what was it with me, letting a tapestry and Winston Churchill cause friction with the one man who was willing to spend his whole life with me? Why did putting sentiment over aesthetic beauty make Peter a freak? Wasn't it natural to hang something on your wall that reminded you of someone you loved?

Sometimes I imagined dumping all of Peter's things in a corner and saying, 'This is your corner.'

Maybe I was trying to help him. Even, 'I don't want you wearing that jacket and looking like a moron.' Future me would cringe every time.

I followed him to the rack of leather jackets, trying to find anything better. I pulled out one but it had fringe, and so I kept looking. Too big, too small.

'Hey, Jake, check out my new jacket.'

'Cool,' Jake said.

'See,' Peter said, 'Jake likes it. I like it and it's cheap and check this out,' he flashed the lining at me, 'It has a world map lining. Isn't that funny?'

'Please don't,' I said. How could I walk down the street with him? Jake watched us. Oh god. Maybe it would be better to let him buy the thing and then accidentally on purpose spill something on it or throw it away, and it would remain a mystery what happened to Peter's great jacket.

'Jake, what do you really think? I don't like it.'

'Well, you know,' Jake said to Peter, 'it's kind of puffy around your waist. Leather should be sleek.' Thank you, Jake! I couldn't believe it; he was helping me. I tried not to smile so as not to rub it in.

'What about this?' I pulled out a suede blazer. Peter tried it on. The colour was a light tan, darker would be better, but it fit him.

'It's nice.' He looked at the price tag. 'But it's forty-five dollars.'

'Peter, that's nothing for a suede blazer.'

'But I want a jacket I can wear every day.'

'You need a new blazer, and besides, there's nothing else here.'

'Actually they do have one, you just don't like it. I'm not like you with your hipster bullshit. I just want a nice leather jacket,' he said. I was his old, fat mother. Was I being an asshole? Why couldn't I just let him buy the fucking thing? Wasn't I a total embarrassment all the time? Wasn't it the least I could do? But I was the one who had to look at the thing.

'But I really do like this blazer,' he said.

Sue showed up, holding a shirt over her arm and a dress with flowers on it. This was a dress you wore for your man to bend you over and bang you. That should be in one of those *Vogue* articles: 'Drive Your Man Crazy by Wearing Clothes for a Wholesome Tween.'

'It fits you so well,' Jake said.

'Yeah,' Sue said. 'But it's not, like, for the winter. I mean, it's just a blazer.' Fuck you, Sue.

'Whatever. I guess forty-five dollars isn't that much, right?' Peter said, eyeing himself in the mirror.

'No, honey, it's nothing if you really like it.'

Disaster averted.

We had to go to dinner at a place with a decent wine list, Peter said. So that left two options, both Italian. We finally picked the closest one. I was covered in sweat again. Peter held my hand. I kind of hated holding hands.

Dinner was a nightmare. An enormous plate of spaghetti with bland marina sauce and a few little pieces of sausage. I tried to eat it, but I couldn't put a dent in it. I pushed the plate forward. Peter and Jake reminisced about some childhood Christmas memory when they were so poor their father had given them each an apple. I didn't understand why they laughed. Something like Stockholm syndrome.

'I'll be right back,' I said, and held up my phone. Peter gave me a dirty look. *I'm thirty years old and an adult, and these people are adults,* I thought. *Why can't I smoke if I want to?*

I turned the corner and stood between two cars on the gravel driveway. I looked up at the sky. Stars. That real pitch-black only found in suburbia or rural areas. No streetlights to brighten up the night. Crickets. The weirdest part of leaving the city was hearing all the sounds you normally didn't hear. I called Amy.

'What's up? Sorry I got off the phone in such a hurry earlier.'

'It's okay. I have food poisoning.'

'Oh god, I'm sorry.'

'Yeah, been puking all day. How are you?'

'We went bowling and to the thrift store. I can't figure out if they like me. I don't know how to talk to people.'

'Everyone likes you.'

'I know, but I have to be a PG-rated version of myself. It's hard for me not to curse and be sarcastic all the time. I don't even know when I'm being sarcastic. I'm so sarcastic all the time.'

'Maybe you'd be better here then, with these fucking weirdos. The sister farted while we were watching *National Lampoon's Vacation,* and then told everyone she had to change her underwear.'

I laughed.

'It wasn't funny. I know it sounds funny,' but she started laughing too. 'How did we end up like this?'

'What do you mean?'

'I mean, Maya, are these really our lives?'

'I know. I wish Peter would just leave me already. I treat him like shit. It's obvious I don't love him. Then I wouldn't be stuck in this rut, and maybe I could, like, have a life.'

'You could never dump people.'

'I know. I just treat them like shit till they leave me, which, if you think about it, is a nice thing to do, because then they can hate you and not feel rejected and sad.'

'Peter's never going to leave you.'

'I know. *As I Lay Dying of Boredom,* that's what my memoir of being married to Peter will be called.'

'Boring is better than a lot of things,' she said.

'No, boring is the worst, because you're, like, 'I'm not being beaten to death; I can live like this,' and then the years go by. You know?'

'I gotta go puke.'

'Seriously?'

'Yeah, honestly, I kind of like puking. It's spiritual for me, like a release of everything.'

'That's beautiful and gross. Take care.'

I looked up at the dark sky over this little shitty town. How did people live in this quiet, where you could hear all of your depressing thoughts? Peter appeared out of nowhere. Where did he come from? How long had he been there? He didn't say anything.

'Hey, honey,' I said, and we kissed.

'Hey, look, they know you smoke.' And before I could say 'What?' Jake and Sue turned the corner.

'It's okay. Sue smoked when I met her,' Jake said, smiling.

'I'm sorry I lied to you guys. I just didn't know how to broach the subject.' I put out the cigarette. Immediately I wanted another.

'Can I bum one?' Sue asked. There was more to Sue than met the eye.

And then the four of us walked down the lonely, quiet street, me and Sue smoking while Jake and Peter walked ahead of us.

Back at house we all stood around the kitchen and retold the day's events. We showed them the things we got at the thrift store. At one point Jake spilled his apple juice on the floor, and I grabbed a dishtowel and wiped it up before Sandy could bend down with her crummy hip.

'So, for Christmas, I want to buy you a winter coat,' Peter's mother said as she handed Peter a catalogue for L.L. Bean.

'Let me see.' I snatched it from him. I started to thumb through it and felt Sue looking with me.

'I really like Jake's coat. Where did he get it?'

'I bought it for him,' she said. 'Where did Peter get those boots?'

'They're Frye boots. I got them for him when we first got together.'

She nodded.

Oh god, we were two little kids dressing up our Ken dolls.

'I like that one,' she said, pointing at an image of a blond-haired man frozen in midwalk with a dog on a mountain path. He was wearing a brown leather bomber.

'Yeah, I wonder if the dog comes with it.'

'I wonder if the man comes with it,' she said in my ear. Sue was an onion peeling itself in front of me.

'I like this one,' I announced.

Peter's mother came over to look at it. 'Oh, honey, five hundred dollars, I don't think we can afford that.' Christ, I had to pick the most expensive thing in the fucking catalogue.

I handed the catalogue back to Peter.

Everyone went to the enclosed porch. They put on a home movie.

In the movie, Peter was swaying in a doorway in blue jeans and a denim jacket, his brown hair falling over his face. 'Whose birthday is it?' his father, holding the camera, asked. 'Gracie's birthday,' Peter said. He was looking at the floor. Then we followed him to Sandy, who was sitting on the ground with fat-faced Gracie among wrapped presents. Jake was sitting Indian style on the floor. 'Open the presents!' he demanded. Gracie was handed one but looked unsure what to do. Jake grabbed it from her and ripped it open. Peter interceded, 'No, let her do it. No! Mom, it's not fair!' Everyone laughed.

The morning after one of my first nights with Peter, we were late and rushing to the bookstore. We huffed up the subway stairs and saw the electronic board indicating our train would arrive in two minutes. 'We don't have to rush,' Peter said, but just then we heard the train come and go before we reached the platform. 'It said two minutes! That was like a second!' Peter yelled. He kicked one of the benches, pissed off. 'It's just not fair,' he said, shaking his head and doing an excellent impression of a bratty kid. I looked at him, baffled. My jaded, calloused heart flopped around, having a seizure. Peter wasn't hardened to the daily frustrations normal grown-ups shrugged their shoulders at while thinking, 'Of course, the board lied, because the world is fucked-up.' Peter's heart was fleshy and pink, and I didn't want anything to hurt it.

Watching other people's home movies was so boring. It was like listening to someone tell you their dream. Who cares, if you're not in it?

'I'm going to bed,' I announced, and went back to the bedroom. Before I turned on the light, I heard someone come in behind me.

'I want you to know I haven't given up on him.'

Rick was standing there.

'How do I turn this on?' I asked, with my fingers on the lamp's neck.

'There's a switch.' I found the switch and clicked it on and turned to face him.

'I wanted you to know. There's still time. Maybe tomorrow in the car on the ride to the train station I can talk to him.'

Two weeks ago, I had called Rick in hysterics about Peter's drinking.

'Okay,' I said.

'Maya, I don't know how to broach the subject without telling him you called me.'

I sat on the bed. 'Look, if you think it will help, I'll tell him.' Peter would kill me, but I couldn't tell his father that, because then it would look like our relationship was fucked-up.

'No, I think you're right. He'll just feel angry, I think.' He eyes scanned the room. 'I don't really know what to do. I've always felt like I failed Peter, you know. I didn't help him find a profession. I could have done better.' Oh god, he was confiding in me. Was I supposed to say it wasn't true? That he had been a great father? That I knew Peter adored him? There was a silence during which I should have said something, but I didn't, and then Rick asked, 'So, how has his drinking been?'

'Better,' I said. I never should have said anything. 'He went through that period of drinking every day, and it was a nightmare, but then he stopped. Probably it was only a phase.' Was it better to justify why I'd called Peter's parents, so they didn't think I was being a drama queen, or to act like I had overreacted, so I wouldn't have to have this awkward conversation? I shouldn't have ever called. Every time you think you should do the right thing, you probably shouldn't do anything. And if we started talking about drinking with Peter, after Peter's rage against me subsided, it would only be a hop and a skip to him telling them about my drug thing. God, I wanted a bag. As soon as I got home. 'Do you think he has a drinking problem?' I asked.

He nodded. 'Yes, I do. I visited him once at college and we went to a grocery store and he bought a bottle of gin at ten in the morning, and I thought, "There's something wrong here."'

What the fuck? He saw his kid buying a bottle of hard alcohol in front of him before breakfast and did absolutely nothing about it? If it had been my mother, the bottle would never have made it to the register. I felt torn between how Peter's and my parents were on opposite sides of the spectrum. Peter's parents only said nice things or nothing; my mother only said awful things all the time. Finally I said, 'If it gets bad again, I'll call you.' Rick left. I popped a Xanax and got into bed.

Even though the whole talk with Peter's dad was awkward, I couldn't help but resent Peter. There was no one asking about me. There was no one whispering about how I was doing, trying to spare my feelings.

What was the difference between Peter drinking and me using? Maybe I resented Peter because his addiction was something legal and mainstream and pretty much accepted. Most people could relate to wanting a stiff drink at the end of the night. People thought hangovers were funny. It was easy for Peter to hide in plain sight with his obvious addiction. *Sideways* was about appreciating wine, not a pathetic alcoholic who stole money from his mother. But no film director wanted to pretend dope wasn't a big deal.

When I drank for the first time at age thirteen, I thought, 'Why don't people do this all the time?' I loved it. I chugged whiskey for fifteen seconds longer than all the boys. But once I discovered dope, alcohol just made me clumsy and dumb and the hangover was so dark. Elizabeth called them 'the creeping fear.' With dope, I could function. It was like wearing armor. You went through the world and nothing could touch you.

Tomorrow night I would be in my own bed with my old problems. I switched off the light. I couldn't sleep. I should have lain there in bed and thought weird thoughts or masturbated. But I didn't. I went back out and joined the others. Everyone had found themselves weirdly awake and wanted to hang out more.

'Why don't we play a game?'

'Why don't we watch a movie?'

And then I unwittingly destroyed everything by suggesting we watch the Netflix film I'd received in the mail the day before. It was about a man who had grown up in a rural town, who brings home his sophisticated girlfriend from the city, who does not fit in. I popped it into the DVD player. Five minutes later, all hell broke loose.

I had seen it in the theaters when it first came out, and I didn't remember anything dirty. But during the opening credits, as the couple was driving to meet the guy's parents, she started rubbing his leg, and then they got frisky while he was trying to drive and he swerved.

Peter's father freaked out. He screamed, 'I think we've seen enough of this ' and turned it off. Then I was faced with two angry, conservative faces. Rick's was red. Sandy looked concerned, as though she wasn't sure I was mentally capable of standing trial. Peter, who had been right beside me, had vanished. 'I didn't remember that,' I said. 'I'm sorry.'

'How could you not remember?' his father screamed. I was not used to other people's parents screaming at me. My own parents had been easy enough. When they'd yelled, I walked away. Sandy shook her head. Jake came to my rescue.

'C'mon, Dad, I'm sure the whole movie isn't like that. Sometimes movies start out like ...' but Rick was pissed. An hour ago we were allies and he was caring and loving, and now he was enraged. My face was frozen in a question mark. I didn't understand. On the edge of my peripheral vision I saw Peter in the bedroom. His back was turned so I couldn't gesture for him to come out and save me. Bastard. I wanted to say, 'That was just the credits. It's not porn.' I didn't say anything except, 'I'm sorry.'

Then anger. I was angry with Peter, who should have shielded me from his parents. I was angry with his parents for making me feel like an asshole. I was angry with the movie. I was mostly angry with myself for suggesting anything. Why put yourself in the line of fire? I was only trying to put on a stupid movie so we could have a fucking pleasant time, and these people were acting like I had ripped up a Bible. Hadn't his father's whole Thanksgiving prayer been about not judging? Didn't Jesus hang out with some whore?

Grace put on a nature documentary. 'I have to go out,' I said, and made Peter come with me.

Outside, I let him have it. 'This is your house. These are your parents. What the fuck? You just leave me there?'

'Why didn't you follow me into the bedroom?' he asked.

'That's weird. You're weird. You were supposed to stand up for me. I didn't know you were going to get up and leave like that! And then I was stuck there and they were screaming.'

'I'm sorry. My dad was being a jerk.'

'I bet they wish I were this white girl with a cross around my neck who has conservative white parents. I will always be, like, "the other."'

'I'm going to talk to him. They were wrong to do that, but they're not racist.' He hugged me. 'Why would you bring that movie?'

'I swear that must be the only sex scene, if you can even call it that. All they showed was a married couple fooling around. How is that unchristian?'

Everyone in the room was an adult, so what was the problem? Was the problem that people made movies like that? I didn't understand who they were fighting for and what the fight was about. The movie had already been made. Sometimes I wished I could have talked to them openly about these ultra-Christian beliefs, just so I could wrap my mind around them.

Sandy left a Post-it on the glass sliding door. 'I'm sorry, but we're prudes.' Wasn't much of an apology.

From then until recorded history ended, I could never recommend a movie again.

I took my last three Xanaxes. Oblivion. Sleep.

—

I sat up and took a long gulp of warm, flat seltzer from the uncapped bottle on the coffee table.

I was going to see Ogden today.

After digging through pockets and looking in books, I found half a bag of dope from the night before. Elizabeth had told me methadone stayed in your system for three to five days and blocked the effects of the dope. Thanksgiving was only three or four days ago. It was a waste to take it.

I snorted two fat lines off an Eastman leather-bound copy of *Moby Dick* with a rolled fifty. I didn't feel less or more like shit.

Peter's father called after we'd gotten back home. He said he was sorry. He had prayed about it, and he realised he shouldn't have judged me. Sandy's fingerprints were all over the phone call. God bless her sweet heart. I imagined her saying, 'You really should call her and apologise.' She probably felt like if she alienated me she would be alienating her own son. It still took a lot for a grown man to call up his son's wife, whom he had been living in sin with before they eloped in Vegas, and say he was sorry. It was like when your mother cried. All of a sudden whatever justification you had for whatever shitty thing you had done disappeared.

After he apologised, there was an awkward silence.

'How are the goats?'

'Great. The mother gave birth. Goats aren't the brightest animals,' he said.

'How dumb are they?' I said, in that cheesy comedian way. He didn't laugh. He thought I was just suddenly talking like a silly man. It really would be better if I stopped talking all together.

Peter appeared in his running shorts with the elastic waistband, the ones that always made me think of his cock somewhere in there, curled up. Men with their stupid balls always hanging there. When they ran, their balls must have bounced a little, and when they peed and shook it, the pee couldn't all come off, so there must always have been little spots of pee on their underwear.

'Love you, hon. Text me and let me know what happened at the doctor's, okay?' he said before he left.

His kiss felt like nothing. The same thing that used to get the serotonin charging through my body left me empty.

'Be back soon.' Door slam. The ring stood in the air for a minute.

Last week I watched Peter stand in front of a mirror and put his sunglasses on different points on his nose for fifteen minutes, and I thought, *This is the person I am spending the rest of my life with.*

I watched Peter pick his nose. I watched Peter really itch his ass, like get all up in there. I watched Peter burn warts off his feet. I watched him spread mayonnaise and hot sauce and peanut butter on a single piece of bread and eat it.

Droplets of sweat ran down Peter's nose as we lay in bed and watched Steve Colbert.

Once, Peter got angry and said he wondered why I didn't get bedsores because he hardly ever saw me move. I knew by the way he said it he had thought it a million times.

The bottom of the bathtub was grimy and sticky because the water took forever to drain. The hot water made me feel cold and then warm. Soaped up my chest and stomach and face. Got soap in my eye. Stung. Imagined the rabbits they tortured *Clockwork Orange*–style with soap just so they knew you couldn't go blind that way. Soaped up my pussy, legs, and ass. Wished I had a cock. I had to rub myself on stuff. Bet it would be fun to jerk off in the shower. Took the razor and put my leg up on the side of the tub, shaved, and then the other one. My sinuses started to clear. I blew snot out of my nose. Shaved the outside of my pussy, covered my clit with a finger and shaved inside at the top where there was always hair and inside the lips and then all the way through the middle and then all inside the ass. Kept feeling with my fingers for those stubborn hairs I had to keep going over. The water felt like someone spitting at me.

The bikini area was a bitch. Ingrown hairs or razor burn. Those lucky bitches back in the seventies could let it all grow out into a giant bush.

Sometimes the present seemed just as dumb as the past if you imagined what it would sound like in the future: *In ancient times the female would rub a bladed tool over her genitalia to slice the hair growing from the body even with the surface of the skin, from where it would grow again.*

I plugged in the laptop and brought it from the coffee table to the couch to watch porn.

The way they characterised the women like different breeds. Black bitch. White cunt. Asian slut.

The line of spit from the cock to the woman's mouth.

A woman blew two guys. When she took them both in her mouth at the same time, the cocks touched. I wondered if that made the men feel a little gay.

A gangbang scene. The men looked pathetic, jerking off as they waited their turn, and then this one dude rubbed his cock in the woman's hair and then wrapped some of her hair around his cock and jerked off with it. Men are so weird.

A girl swallowed and then opened her mouth and stuck out her tongue so you could see she really did swallow it all.

An asshole, a wrinkled, gaping hole spitting back the come like an awful little volcano, and you thought to yourself, 'Why would anyone on earth want to see that?' And yet there it was. Someone on earth wanted to see just that.

The men were bullies. Pulling, slapping, ordering the women around.

I put the throw pillow underneath me and started to fuck it.

I liked watching the scenes where the women really didn't look like they wanted it. Like they were just doing it for the money or drugs or whatever.

When I came, I came wanting it all. In one way or another, I wanted to be the men, and I wanted to hurt the woman. I wanted to hurt like the woman, and I wanted to hate the men for hurting me. I wanted to be the man at home jerking off wanting to be the man wanting to hurt the woman. And then I wanted to hurt more.

Wasn't it a little sad we couldn't do a little of everything there is to do? I would never know what it felt like to jam my cock into a tight little asshole.

I woke up and looked at the clock to see how late I was. Every time I looked at a clock, I hated myself. I grabbed my iPod, threw it in my purse, put on my big purple sunglasses, and ran out and got into a cab. Put my headphones on. Lucinda Williams sang, 'Lemon trees don't make a sound.' Then the iPod died.

Should have showered after I masturbated. My jeans rubbed against my shaved pussy and made me feel wet and gross.

In high school I went down on a girl at a party in a field. Her hairy, gnarly pussy on my face and the pussy juice all running down my neck. It tasted like pennies.

After I stood there forever, smoking cigarettes and calling Ogden's phone and getting sent to voicemail, Ogden finally turned the street corner. It always felt like he came out of nowhere, like it was some kind of magic trick when he appeared.

He said he was sorry. He looked like he hadn't slept in a hundred years. It felt nice to be pressed against the cool leather of his jacket. When love came easy, it felt like it would last forever.

'What's wrong?'

'What do you mean?' he asked. He took out a pack of American Spirits. 'Want to smoke?'

'Sure,' I said. I tried smiling. My teeth felt soft.

We walked down the street. When his hand came near mine I held it, but then he pulled his away and put it in his jacket pocket.

Robert Lowell wrote, 'What woman has the measure of man / who only has to care about himself / and follow the stars' / extravagant, useless journey across the sky... / Because they cannot love, they need no love.' The stars didn't need anything. Men did, though. Just because they couldn't love didn't mean they didn't need love. They needed more, usually.

The first time I spent the night with Ogden, I lay on the sofa drinking wine while he hung paintings. All of the paintings looked as much like nothing as you could think of. He stepped back and asked me if one was crooked. I asked him if I could watch television, and he said, 'Whatever.'

Sometimes I thought the only natural ending to our relationship would be a homicide/suicide. Anything else would feel like a letdown.

The first night I stayed at his apartment, I passed out at some point. I woke up in the middle of the night on the couch, freezing. The streetlight shone through a window. I couldn't find the light switch. I walked down the hallway with my hand against the wall. The floor was cold. I woke him up by punching him in the shoulder. 'How do you leave me on the sofa with no blanket or sheet or pillow or anything? Why didn't you wake me up and take me to bed?'

'Sorry,' he mumbled into the pillow.

'Is this your first day on Earth?' I asked him. I found the light, which made him sit up with his eyes squinting. He picked up his glasses from the bedside table, like, *Let me put these glasses on so I can deal with this bullshit.* He asked me to lower my voice. How many times in my life was someone asking me to lower my voice?

'I came here so we could spend some quality time, not to watch you hang up paintings and then leave me passed out on the sofa. This is the most boring masochistic thing ever.'

'Maybe I didn't want to deal with whatever crisis you have this week and then have sex with you. I am an actual person,' he said.

'I'm an actual person too. Not a thing you leave on a sofa, for Chrissake. And why is this fucking house so cold?' And then I broke down crying. Then there was silence, and I said, 'I want a father figure, not an actual replacement for my actual father who actually neglected me. This isn't Freudian. It is retarded.'

We went to a bistro on Eighty-First and Park. He asked the host about sitting at the bar, but I said I wanted a table and pointed to the corner booth, only for the host to walk us past it.

'That's a four top,' Ogden explained. We had a choice between three different tables.

'Want to hide behind the column?' he asked.

'Sure,' I said.

'Do you want to hear the specials?' the waitress asked. He didn't answer. She picked up the specials menu and pointed at each item while she read it out loud. After she left, he looked at me and said, 'What the fuck was that about? She read what was on the menu.'

'How's your dog?' I asked.

Ogden went on about his car breaking down instead. All the crying messages I had left for him echoed in my head. I wanted to run out of the restaurant and throw myself into traffic.

'The car broke down and I had the dog and the cat with me and I had to take them to a motel …'

We stood outside smoking after we ate and ordered another round of drinks. It looked like it was going to rain. I had always loved dismal weather. I found it comforting. I wrapped my arms around him.

'Let's go back to your place,' I said.

He stared at me.

'Do you have any pot? I want to get stoned and do it,' I said, almost whining.

'No, I don't think you should come back with me tonight.'

'Why not?'

'I think we should cool it for a while.'

'Why? Peter doesn't know anything, I swear.'

He shook his head. 'That's not it.'

'What did I do?'

'You didn't do anything.'

'When did you decide this?'

'A while ago.'

'We can't just fuck?'

'Nope.'

'We can't even make out?'

'No.'

'Do you love me?' I asked.

'No,' he said. Extras passed us by, glancing at us. What was the storyline they imagined? That old man was hurting that young woman.

'What the fuck are you talking about?' My voice rose.

'I'm not being cryptic.'

'You never did?'

'Why do you think I never said it back to you?'

'I thought you didn't want to confuse everything because I'm married.'

'I'm sorry, I thought you knew.'

'Do you care that I love you?'

He looked at me like I should have already known the answer. He looked at me like he didn't want to have to say it, and then he said it. 'No.' Right on cue: the lump in my throat and the tears down my face. He looked at me like he really didn't want to be going through this bullshit right now.

'Are you attracted to me?' I asked. Throw me a fucking bone.

'Not as much as I probably should be.'

'What the fuck are you talking about?'

He opened the door for some woman with a stroller to come out and then nodded at me. 'Let's go back inside.'

We sat down. I cried. There was no point in trying to hold it together anymore.

This is life: You walk down this path and people join you. Then they leave, and you're alone again, and you keep replacing them. Then those people leave too.

'I don't want to be with you. You need to accept that,' he said.

'I learned it a second ago,' I said.

'Look, I'm not abandoning you. I do care about you.' This was part of the speech he had rehearsed so he could come out as clean as possible. So he could say to himself, 'I didn't just abandon her.'

'Are you seeing someone?'

'There isn't another woman,' he said.

'Give me another chance.'

'Believe me, it's better if it ends like this than if we had a big blowup or if Peter found out. This way we can always be friends, okay?' He smiled.

'I thought you loved me.'

'I didn't love you and I never have,' he said, staring directly into my eyes. 'I didn't chase you. I didn't lie to you.' He was being a lawyer. He had all this evidence. 'I never said I loved you or made you any promises. I've always been honest with you.'

'Stop it. Look, I only like to be treated badly in a hot way.'

'I'm sorry, but I'm not your husband. I didn't make any vows to you.'

'You're a great teacher, by the way. Some of the lessons were repetitive, like what a giant fucking asshole you are.'

'You came on to me!'

'Right, the innocent sixty-one-year-old teacher who was taken advantage of. Ripped from the headlines of *Asshole Magazine*.' My voice got louder. People were staring. I was officially making a scene.

'I only answer you when you text or email me first.'

'Like that proves anything except how fucked-up you are. You led me on and you know it.'

'Fine, I wanted you then but now I don't. Clear?' He blinked and then he glared at me. I could feel him hating me for not going along with the script. I wasn't supposed to fight back. I was supposed to cry and say I understood.

'If you never heard from me again, would you care?' Fuck it. If he wasn't going to have sex with me, then what was the point of trying to be cool about this?

'I would be concerned.'

'Concerned like they're out of milk at the store, or concerned like my child is missing?'

'In the middle,' he said.

'Why did you start with me?' I should have shut up and left.

There were no answers that would make anything better.

He shrugged. 'It was a long time ago.'

'How is it possible I'm sitting here dying, and you're sitting there like nothing?'

He shook his head. 'We're living in two different universes.'

'Did you sleep with other people when we were together?'

'Yeah.'

'Why didn't you tell me?'

'Because it was none of your business.'

'What do you want?'

'I want to be with someone I can be with *be with*. Someone I can marry.'

'But you're old and completely fucked-up. Why would anyone want you?'

'Great point. Why did you want me?'

'Because I could tell you were sad.'

'I wasn't.'

'Can't you, like, grandfather me in to this new life of yours? Fuck me till you find a wife?'

'Grandfather you in? You're funny,' he smirked. 'C'mon, let's be friends. This is the worst.' He never said anything was 'the worst' before he met me. He was using my own language to manipulate me into not making a scene. He deserved to be embarrassed.

The waitress came by, and I asked for a dessert menu. I was making it uncomfortable for him by making him sit there. I was willing to endure the pain knowing at least I was making this difficult for him.

'Will you share with me?' I asked.

'Sure,' he said.

I ordered the triple chocolate mousse and banana ice cream. 'You are a deceitful selfish asshole.'

'You're the one who is married, and I'm the one who's deceitful?'

That was good. I hated him. I kind of wanted to make out with him. Why was he doing this? Why couldn't we just go and fuck and be happy?

'I'm married, so I'm always the villain and you're always the innocent one, right?'

He grinned. 'Why did you want an old guy like me anyway?'

I could tell it wasn't an act. Never seeing me again didn't mean shit to him. Take that, self-esteem. 'Is this the only way you can get off anymore?'

'Keep it up, and I'm gone,' he said.

'Fine, go. I'll go, actually. You are officially boring the shit out of me.'

I stood up and threw my napkin in his face and knocked over my water. Before I could take his glass and throw it at him, he jumped out of his seat, and then I left. Tears running down my cheeks. I called Elizabeth on the phone. I was blubbering. She said, 'Just come here.'

Behind every crazy woman is a man sitting very quietly, saying, 'What? I'm not doing anything.'

—

It was inevitable from the moment we met that Peter would leave me.

After we returned from visiting his family, things cooled between us. It was obvious, but he wouldn't admit to anything being different. A common tactic of men – denying they are behaving differently so you feel like you're just going nuts.

He would wake up early, go for a run, do sit-ups as he watched *The Colbert Report,* then go to work, and then come home. Instead of watching anything with me like he normally did, he would pass out facing the wall. I tried to kiss him but would get a cheek instead of his lips. When I said, 'I love you,' he said it back like a robot. When I asked him what was wrong, he said he was busy. I chose to believe him.

We had been together for so long we had gone through cycles, and I wanted to believe this was just another one. I tried waiting it out. There would be a day when he would feel lonely or sad and then he would come to me. If I pushed too hard it would just start a fight. He would scream, 'Dammit, Maya, I am exhausted.'

I called Ogden. 'Hey, miss me?'

'Of course.'

'Regret dumping a hot piece of ass since you know you're closer to death, and you probably won't have that many chances to have sex?'

'Every moment of the day.'

'Good. Drinking more?'

'Yeah, Maya, I'm completely miserable and live in constant regret.'

'It's too bad you ruined a good thing. You'll never get another chance.'

'I don't think I could honestly live with myself if I lost you again, so maybe it's better we don't try it again.'

'What level is your sarcastic meter up to?' I asked.

'It's so high it's almost full circle back to being earnest.'

'I don't have time for your old man mind games. It's kind of a waste talking to you anyway, since you probably won't remember anything because, you know, you're old and probably getting senile. Thank god I won't have to be there when you have ranch dressing running down your wrinkled varicose-veined chin.'

'All your jokes and comments about me getting old and senile never get old.'

'That's because you don't remember them because you're old and senile.'

'This is tiresome and frustrating.'

'Yeah, that's what you're going to be saying when you're trying to bang a woman your own age.'

'Maya, seriously, I have work to do.'

'Peter is being weird. Like not talking to me or touching me. Ever since we got back from Vermont. I think he's going to leave me.'

'You're the one who might be having memory issues. How many times did you say to me you needed to get out of your marriage? That you were stuck in a rut?'

'That's different from him leaving me. I was talking about me leaving him.'

'So leave him. You're unhappy with him, you need to get your life back together. Why don't you ask him to take a break?'

'A break? That's stupid. I'm not ready. It was one thing when I had you, but if he leaves … I'm just not ready. I need to line up another dude.'

'Why can't you be alone for five minutes?'

'I probably have some kind of personality disorder. I can spend hours alone watching television or listening to music. But being sober, the silence creeps up. I can't handle it. I can't handle not having someone around to tell me I look hot or get mad at me or just generally acknowledge my existence. It's like, what's the point of being alive if no one is there to see it? If there's no one to disapprove of my behavior, then why bother doing it?'

'Your dance card won't be empty for very long.'

'God, a new one. Find a new dude, fall in love, and then slowly start to see whatever special, unique fucked-up hell starts to show itself. Everyone is fucked-up. It's just a matter of waiting to see what kind it is and if you can put up with it. At least Peter keeps the kitchen clean. He is a good wife.'

'Maya, I have to go.'

'What are you doing?'

'I'm reading.'

'You mean the old-timey way, with the paper and the binding and stuff?'

'Yes, Maya, with my magnifying glass because of my old, fucked-up eyes, in my wheelchair, with my catheter bag.'

'Aww, thanks, I needed that. Your body used to function, and now it's all fucked-up. Anyway, back to my life. Can you tell me what I can do to get Peter back and then find another dude and then dump him?'

'Go away for a few days, that might work.'

'What if when he's alone he realises he likes being alone better than being with me?'

'If there's any chance of him staying with you, I'm telling you, leaving for a week or two is the best way to get him back.'

'So, you don't think crying, threatening suicide, and throwing a nonstop tantrum is the way to go?'

'As cute as you look blubbering with spit and tears all over your face, I would say not this time.'

'It usually works when I want him to buy something and we're in public.'

'I gotta go, Maya, seriously.'

'You sure you don't want me to come over? I'll give you a BJ.'

'I wish. Not right now. I need to get out from under this pile of papers. I keep waiting for the elves to do it.'

'So basically my amazing blow jobs don't top the amount of crazy bitch you have to put up with.'

'Maya, you're not a crazy bitch.'

'God, Ogden, you actually sound sincere when you say that. But then again, you're so fucking nuts, compared to you I am probably sane.'

'Thanks, Maya. Any time I need to feel a little more shitty about myself, I know who to call.'

'No problem! Love you! Bye!'

I didn't leave for a week like Ogden suggested. I didn't cry and threaten suicide. I went on OkCupid and started dating. I made out with a dork outside a bar. I did coke in a bathroom with a man who allegedly worked in finance but actually worked at a movie theater and had a fake, ambiguously European accent. I never liked coke, but it was something. I learned the world was full of dudes I had absolutely nothing to say to. Peter wasn't special, but at least we could have a conversation.

Once we had kids everything would be about raising the kids, and then we would be too old to fuck anyway. I waited patiently for the first day off he would have in a week.

I crawled out of bed and found Peter on the sofa watching television, dipping French fries into a mix of rooster sauce and mayo. Peter loved mayo. Gross.

'Peter, what the fuck is going on? Please tell me.'

He turned off the television. 'I've been looking at apartments and I found one.'

'You found what? An apartment?'

I could already feel the metaphorical luggage of Peter's leaving weighing me down, fucking up my back, turning me into one of those sad, shitty people who hunch over, don't look up, and walk around with their plastic bags full of weird things.

He hadn't caught me cheating. I hadn't done dope since we got back from Vermont except for that one time, and Peter had no clue. I bought a bundle before we left, ten bags, but since I had gone through withdrawal during the trip, I realised the hard part was over, and I didn't want to go back to doing it every day, figuring out how to get the money and the whole hassle. I put the eight bags between the mattresses. When I didn't have a supply I was desperate, but as long as I had those eight bags, I wasn't using because I didn't have any; I could use whenever I wanted. It was a choice. When I was fiending I would look at them. I would think about ripping them open and doing it, but then I would think about how I knew exactly how it would feel, and then I didn't have to do it. It felt like more of a high not to get high. I thought AA and NA were bullshit because they were all about things having power over you, but one of the things you learn when you starve yourself is that your mind can actually power off your body's biological need to survive. If I could deny my body what it needed, then there was no doubt I could stop using. I could beat it. I wouldn't let it take any space or time in my real life. Drugs were for fun or true moments of crisis.

This was a true moment of crisis. In my mind I had already ripped opened two bags and snorted them as fast as possible and was leaning back, closing my eyes, waiting for that wall of soothing numbness to hit. I stared at Peter. His mouth was moving and he was saying words like, 'friends', 'love', 'sorry', 'hopeful', 'wishing', and more words that sounded kind, but I knew if I actually listened to him then the words would feel like glass shards slowly tearing my skin. *Yeah, Peter. Sure, I'll play along. This is all reasonable.* I nodded. 'Oh yeah, that makes sense,' I said, because I was in opposite world, where nothing made sense. Peter leaving me? He was the dude who didn't leave. Who promised over and over he wouldn't leave. What the fuck?

Yeah, I'm the girl who lost the boy *after* she stopped using drugs and ended her extramarital affair.

'You know I stopped using.'

'I'm so proud of you, but that doesn't change anything,' he said, rubbing my shoulder.

Proud of me? I wanted to take the ashtray and bash his face with it. It would have been better if he had said, 'Here is all the money I have. You can have it, because what I'm doing is fucked-up. It's assumed because I married you I wouldn't say out of the blue that I'm leaving you, since that's what marriage is. Since I have no words to offer, I will give a bunch of money.' That was the least he could do. But words were all he had. Stupid dumb words that didn't mean shit to me.

'I'll be right back,' I said. I got the bags and *The Bell Jar* (a little on the nose but whatever) from the bedroom and went back to the living room. I did the two bags off the coffee table in front of him because what the fuck was the difference?

He kept talking in that nice way of his about how he had tried and how it was nobody's fault. He sighed and said, 'We can stop pretending.' What the hell did that mean? He had been pretending? He had tears in his eyes. He was serious.

'What do you mean, pretending?'

'Didn't it feel like we were going through the motions?'

'No, I love you, and you're leaving me for no reason.'

He stared directly at me with tears running down his face, and said, 'Fuck you. This is what you wanted.'

What the fuck was he talking about? I wondered, after I slowly came to from binge watching *Don't Trust the B---- in Apartment 23* and doing all the dope I had. I had completely lost my tolerance and kept nodding out. I would jerk awake and find myself bent over, my head almost touching the floor. It sounded like Peter was dragging shit across the bedroom floor.

This is what you wanted. Oh. What I said to Amy on the phone. 'I wish Peter would just leave already. I'm never going to dump him, and all I do is treat him like shit.' He must have overheard me when I was smoking outside. My stupid mouth saying stupid things. Had I even meant it? *Was this exactly what I wanted?* I snorted another bag. No more being scared that the biggest thrills left for me were buying things at Crate & Barrel. I was free. Anything and nothing could happen.

In the future everyone will ask me, 'Why did your marriage end? What did *you* do?'

Peter and I walked over to Elizabeth's. She sold me five bars of Xanax and gave me a hug. She was strung out. Her apartment told the story. All the lights were off and there was a candle and her laptop was playing a show with no laugh track. I wanted to stay, but Peter was outside waiting.

I'd never learned how to get dumped. I didn't know how to not take it personally.

'Peter, I didn't mean it. I didn't mean any of it. I'm not pretending. I love you.'

141

'No, Maya, you did mean it. All you do is push yourself away from me. I can feel it.'

'It's scary to emotionally depend on someone.'

'It's supposed to be hard. That's why it means something, and that's why it never meant anything to you,' he said.

'You don't want to be alone, Peter, c'mon.'

'Maya, I started looking as soon as we got back, and I've already put the deposit down.'

'Where is it?'

'Bushwick.'

'That's what fucking happens. You fall in love, and in one way or another you end up in metaphorical or literal Bushwick. This place of just total shit.'

'I'd rather live in Bushwick than here,' he said.

This human being would rather get drunk in a shitty apartment in fucking Bushwick and risk dying alone than be with me.

One day I'll be strong enough, I thought. *One day I'll just go and jump off a bridge.*

The following weeks were the opposite of a blur. Raw and sharp. I cried so much I didn't even know what I was crying about. I forgot to eat. Dread was the first thing I felt when I opened my eyes. Peter gave me money all the time, and I took Xanax and heroin all the time. We both knew it was the only way he would get any sleep.

I told him I would kill myself, because no one was allowed to just leave someone like that. He didn't respond. Was I actually going to have to kill myself to prove a point?

I looked out the window at a child wearing an oversized book bag in the courtyard, waiting for the bus. There was a world where kids went to schools, and the postal service mailed letters so people could communicate, and there were train conductors conducting trains and buses picking people up so they could get from one place to another, and there were nurses using wet Q-tips to moisten the lips of people in comas, and people who volunteered to cradle babies who didn't have parents. And there were wars, and people died. And I was always in a room, crying.

I lost my job at the bookstore. This douchebag had shown up, who was supposed to be the one to supervise textbooks but was put in charge of the whole staff instead. This made Michelle quit. And then one by one, he fired everyone. We had all been friends, and now we were like a slowly dying family. We talked a lot of smack, but no one actually wrote nasty letters to the owners. No one quit. We each waited our turn. We looked at the douchebag's blog and laughed at him for being a Dungeons & Dragons enthusiast and groaned at what an awful human being he was. In one post he wrote, 'Had to fire a girl today. But she couldn't get with the program.' He said things like, 'Get with the program.' People who worked there for years were booted and replaced by eighteen-year-old girls the douchebag called 'sweetheart.'

I don't know why it is that when some men call you 'sweetheart' or 'honey,' it makes you blush, yet when other men do it, you want to hurl.

There was no order or reason to it. He fired everyone, the hard working along with the lazy. After the firings got underway, every time a customer asked about a book, I would go on Amazon and show them how much cheaper they could buy it from there.

I stole everything I could get my hands on.

I watched everyone get replaced before the email arrived at two in the morning informing me I didn't need to bother coming in the next day.

I looked on craigslist for jobs.

I finally landed a temp job at a labor union in the East Twenties. The middle-aged man who interviewed me leered. He asked me personal questions ('Do you live alone, or?'), made stunted small talk ('I used to live in the city ...'), and periodically checked to see if my breasts were still where they were the last time. He was cross-eyed, so he could check on both. He was one of those old, gross men who went through life trying to muster the courage to commit to sexually harassing someone instead of just being a slimy perv.

I took the place of a woman who had kept a calendar with cats that had very unoriginal things to say about Mondays.

Boys wearing headphones inhabited the beige cubicles dividing the office floor. Nobody talked. I wanted work to be around people. But I was always alone there.

I told Peter to pack while I was at work, but he didn't. He did it right in front of me instead. He stood in front of the bookshelf with his eyes squinted, looking for his books. When we got married, we threw out duplicate copies of the books we owned.

'Just give me the shittier pots and pans, but don't take them all,' I begged him. He told me I should have felt lucky he was taking as little as he was. He didn't have to be nice anymore. It really didn't fucking matter what we said or did to each other now.

All the best memories suddenly rematerialised the moment he told me he was leaving. Those fuzzy memories of the beginning. Going to the beach, laughing in bed, making love while Steve Earle blared on the stereo. The way he always held the umbrella to completely cover me. The human mind plays the worst tricks.

Everyone thought his leaving was the right thing. 'Just let him go. Believe me, it's a blessing,' Ogden said.

I did dope in the bathroom at least three times a day.

Somehow along the way my sleeve snagged. Using was my life. Not using was my life. One or the other, I couldn't get out of the cycle. Everything revolved around it. My life became myopic. I could only use or not use. I could never be totally free from the whole fucking thing.

It wasn't like it slowly happened. It wasn't something that gradually took over my life. But when Peter left I thought to myself, *Just be a junkie now.*

Get high all the time. Why not? Pure hedonistic joy, and then when I found a man, I would clean up for him.

Sometimes I stretched out in bed reading books. Sometimes I wrote poetry. Sometimes I tried on clothes. Sometimes I cleaned the whole apartment and ate a pint of ice cream.

Douglass, Elizabeth's ex, moved in right after Peter left. Douglass was in his fifties, and I had never liked him, but anything was better than being alone. He walked like a caveman, spoke in deep voice, and used big words just to make you feel dumb. He had always been dismissive of me. But once I gave him a free place to live, I started seeing what Elizabeth saw in him. He could be kind. He would make me food. He would come back after disappearing for hours with cookies or a bag of oranges. Women swooned over him. He had a ripped body, even though the only exercise he got was walking to and from a drug dealer. The grey in his dreads didn't age him; it really did make him look distinguished. He wore beat-up jeans that hung from his hips. He had spent his life being supported by some poor girl who had really thought she could change him. As long as I had money, he didn't mind running for me.

A runner is someone who goes out to score you drugs. The reasons people have runners are: they don't have a connection themselves, they don't want to take the risk of scoring and walking around with dope actually on them, or they are lazy. Normally, you pay a runner twenty bucks, which is two bags. I bought Douglass more than I should have for running. If I didn't, he would just steal more of my bags.

Amy had sent me a five-hundred-dollar check. Ogden sent me a grand. Everyone sent me money because they felt bad, and it all went up my nose, not to mention the money from my job. I barely looked at food. Whenever I did eat a cookie or a slice of pizza my body would ache for more, but I wanted to be skinny almost more than I wanted to get high.

There was a guy, one of the cubicle boys with the headphones, who made the mistake of flirting with me. He took me to lunch. I came in the next day and got so high, I told him I was high. Later that night he texted me to leave him alone forever.

Peter was gone. Ogden was gone. They just kept leaving.

'This is what you wanted,' my psychiatrist reminded me. I knew I had sat in that office with those plants I was pretty sure were fake (I kept reminding myself to touch them to see) and said how much better off I would be if we broke up. But there had always been a part of me that got off on shit talking Peter. It was a kind of showing off: look, I can have this thing and not even care I have it. Having a man wasn't everything when you had a man. Maybe I took him for granted, or maybe he was kind of shitty. I couldn't remember.

'I just want to die,' I wailed to Douglass as he was putting on his shoes to go score for me.

Douglass and I watched movies constantly and got high till we passed out. Sometimes Douglass made food. One time, he did the laundry. He never showered. His body reeked of musk, and it was like a cartoon stink cloud followed him. He left dishes right on the floor in front of the couch. He left syringes without caps on the sofa, the floor, in piles of garbage. When someone was supposed to come over, I would scan the room and de-syringe it, fuming with rage at how stupid and dangerous he could be. If we had had a pet, it would be dead.

I chain-smoked in a thin black slip and slippers. I was content in my bubble. Nothing in this bubble could hurt me, if you didn't count me. Life was going to be awesome and awful, beautiful and ugly. The most exciting things that were going to happen to me would not be anywhere near Crate & Barrel. They would be in bars and streets and dark places. I would wake up in bright places and laugh at sad things and cry over dumb things. I would never get married again. I would never get stuck.

—

The first time I had sex after Peter was with a woman, in front of the man who had paid me.

I had always looked at those ads on craigslist. Sugar daddy ones. I already liked older men. I was kind of a masochist. I loved sex. I needed money. So what if there was a male counterpart who wanted to spoil me? To treat me like a little girl? Sure, it sounded a little creepy. But creepy things turned me on.

Someone said to me once, 'Don't ever think with your crotch.'
    I was going to think with my crotch. I wanted to feel hot

and have men buy me shit. That could be a life, right? That could be a pretty cool life.

The first time I was nervous. He told me his name was Brian. He sounded normal enough: lived in Connecticut, married, two kids. A daughter my age. I lied and said I was twenty-five. I could have passed for younger but decided not to push it. His voice was nasal, and his picture was a vacation picture of him on a ship wearing a loud shirt. He looked so corny. I went back and forth with Douglass about whether or not to do it. Safety-wise it seemed all right: condoms and a hotel room. The only advice Douglass gave me was not to invite anyone from craigslist over to the apartment. Hotels seemed safe. A lot of people saw you. If you screamed bloody murder, someone would probably hear you.

I felt better when Brian said there would be another girl. She went to Columbia. He saw her regularly. Could both of them be weirdo psychos, like the couple that abducted that Jaycee Lee Dugard girl? Probably not. Then he texted that he had a third girl. I would be one of three girls, meaning a lot less of the actual action and safety in numbers. He hadn't seen this other girl before either.

'I'm not normally like this. I don't want you to think I just have three girls at once. This is so rare, like the moon aligned with the stars or something.'

Douglass was going to come with me in a cab and stand around like an extra so he could get a look at the guy, and then he would wait at a Starbucks nearby. If something shady went down, I would text 'O.K.,' and then we weren't sure what. Douglass said he would call the police at that point, because what was one dude going to do?

I never actually anticipated that Brian would be pretty hot. He didn't look like his picture. He was wearing an expensive suit. His smile was disarming. He moved his hands when he talked, like Woody Allen.

There was no way the Columbia girl was twenty-two, but who the hell was I to out her?

He brought five condoms. She said, 'You wish you could use all of those.'

'I know,' Brian said. 'I do. One and I'm done. That's what happens when you get to be my age.'

I went to the bathroom and turned on the water. I did a line and then another. Then I realised I wasn't sure I was going to be alone again. I did most of the bag.

The Columbia girl told me her story while we smoked a cigarette outside. 'I was just checking out the ads. So I answered one, and then I met him at a Starbucks, but I couldn't go through with it, so I actually just bailed on him. But he kept insisting I meet him again, so I did, and then I don't know. He doesn't take long. And he's okay.'

Brian kissed me. It felt awkward while the other girl was there. She wasn't that pretty.

I cuddled with him in bed. He felt my hair. He unbuttoned his shirt. He told me to suck his nipples. It felt oddly feminine to be sucking on a nipple.

The third girl was a trip. She was Puerto Rican. She walked in talking on the phone, loud as hell. 'Yeah, this white dude, I'm here now, Julio, lemme get down to business.' She plugged in her phone and turned up the clock radio. Brian muttered something about his hearing and the horrible music. She didn't care. She introduced herself as Liberty. I giggled. I was getting wasted on the wine Brian had brought.

Liberty came out of the bathroom in a crazy getup. She had a belly she was not ashamed of. Suspenders went over her tits and then clipped onto garters. A crazy booty and a tongue ring. She targeted me. Reeked of vanilla, which made me hungry and nauseous. She started sucking my tits and made a big show out of biting my nipples. Brian stood there with the white girl going down on him.

I was on all fours with this girl licking my ass and finger-banging the shit out of me. I was screaming.

I played with her pussy, but it was so obvious I didn't know what I was doing. She removed my hand and said, 'Let me.'

Brian wanted to see Liberty go down on the Columbia girl. I went to the bathroom and did another line. When I got back to the room, Brian was lying down and the Columbia girl was going down on him. I felt oddly competitive when he said she gave the best head ever. He asked me and Liberty to suck on his nipples.

'This is fucking awesome,' he said over the blare of the clock radio playing some actively annoying song with a techno beat.

Then I went down on him, but he wasn't making the same sounds as he had with the Columbia girl. I wanted to be awesome at giving head. I was going to have work on that. He looked directly at me and asked Liberty to go down on him.

Liberty got between his legs.

'Hey, no teeth!'

'Sorry, I like it rough,' she said.

'I said no teeth!'

'That's the way I do ' she said.

'That's better,' he said. 'Okay, now stop.'

But she didn't stop and he grunted.

All that money and five condoms and this dude got off from a BJ after five minutes of getting head.

He said it was late anyway, and he had to get home. 'Nothing like young women to make you feel alive.' I felt bad for his wife, as though I was part of a mean private joke he played on her. I hoped she killed him one day and got away with it.

I got three hundred bucks for forty minutes of accumulated action.

'Do you do this a lot?' I asked Liberty.

'Well, since I got out.'

'Got out?'

'Yeah, I was locked up for smoking crack,' Liberty said.

'Someone named Liberty wasn't free,' I said, cracking myself up.

I gave Douglass the money and told him to call the dude. Douglass said the guy was going to stop by in the morning. But he didn't stop by the next day, or the day after. Three days we waited for him. The cash was on the bookshelf underneath a heavy statue of a girl with her eyes closed. We had the money, and there was nothing on Earth we could do to make the dope get there any faster. It was the same feeling I had when I was in a cab, late, stuck in traffic. No matter how much money you have in your wallet the cab doesn't move.

We grumbled and watched terrible movies. Douglass was king of the remote. I was too weak to put up a fight. I didn't want to be alone, but being around Douglass wasn't much better. I tried to cuddle with him, but he said, 'I can't do this cuddling thing right now, babe.' Sweat was making my body rot. I rubbed between my tits where there was a little puddle of sweat. I smelled it. There was something sickly comforting in the smell of hotdogs and sweat. I wiped underneath my left tit and rubbed off a thin layer of skin.

Douglass decided to try to score out on the street. This was an act of desperation. If you got busted, it almost always happened when you scored on the street. That's why I only dealt with delivery guys. I didn't want him to go, but the dealer wasn't even answering our texts. I gave him all my money. Douglass's phone was broken, so there wasn't going to be any way of getting ahold of him. Our plan was not a very good plan.

I tried to embrace getting clean so I would never be in this position again, dope sick, lying on my unwashed sheets, and thinking, *Finally, it's over. Finally, I will be clean, and this whole stupid ordeal will be over.* I sobbed.

You have to be tough to be a drug addict. You have to sit there a lot of the time and be sick. So many times I thought, *I am not too much of a wuss to be a drug user.*

The true mark of any addict is the ability to deal with being dope sick. Some people chain-smoked and paced around and made frequent trips to the bathroom to shit or puke. Other people were silent and looked for ways to busy themselves. I methodically went through the ashtray, putting aside butts with some tobacco left. Later, Douglass would roll cigarettes using these stale bits of tobacco. Douglass stared at the television. We were the weird people in a waiting room. In every waiting room there is a loony, and I was that loony.

Douglass, being a seasoned junkie, was the calm one. 'You just have the flu. Imagine you have the flu. It's only a matter of time. Do you think we will never score again?'

I didn't tell him I had Suboxone, which I had been taking over the last two days.

You can't be junkies and be friends. To be a junkie means constantly choosing yourself over anyone else. And it's hard not to grow resentful when you are paying for someone else's habit.

At our worst, Douglass was a parasite feeding off my sickness. At our best, we were a team, a tag team of vultures. We lied to one another all the time. 'I lost my fucking bag. It was right there. Can I have one of yours?' Douglass stole from me. I heard him open my dope drawer while I was pretending to sleep, and when I sat up he shut it quick. We would talk about our broken hearts, our lives, our plans. But there was always a line. I would let him be sick if it meant I could be high.

Douglass shocked me when he came back within half an hour with no drugs but almost all the money. It was twenty short. 'I had to buy a drink,' he said as he sank into the sofa. There was still a hundred, so we had enough for a bundle.

The rash underneath my tit had gotten worse. Flaps of skin kept flaking off. My head grew sweaty and when I rubbed it, dirt gathered under my nails. My stomach felt caught in-between vomiting and shitting. The eggs Douglass had made the morning before smelled pungent but not entirely unappealing. How could he sit there and eat an apple? Had he spent twenty bucks on two bags for himself? Had he shot up in the bar bathroom? Had he thought what I didn't know wouldn't hurt me?

Had he thought since he was the one who could have gotten busted, he deserved a couple bags? It didn't matter. I wasn't going to accuse him. Twenty bucks for a drink in a shitty bar? I stared at the phone. I kept rereading the texts. I tried to come up with some kind of timeline. One hour ago he said he'd be here in twenty minutes, so maybe twenty minutes meant two hours. Even if he had left when he had texted twenty minutes, he had to be here in two hours. I kept imagining him driving around the corner, parking, walking down the steps and through the courtyard, expecting him to buzz right then.

Right then.

Right then.

The buzzer kept not buzzing.

I kept going to the bathroom. I shit like ten times in a day.

I sat there hating myself. Hating the room. Hating the smells. Hating the discarded Snapple wrapper. Hating seeing that same crumpled brown bag on the floor. Hating that I never picked it up.

I mostly hated this fucking movie Douglass put on about this sad, quirky boy in some small town who fell in love with a quirky girl who was a carnie, and she made him less of a wuss. I fucking hated watching two people fall in love, and I hated thinking of Peter, Peter, Peter. How many fucking memories were there, and I did have to individually grieve each one? Why couldn't I just put them all in one big box and throw them away like he did?

I hated thinking of Peter. Peter driving at night while I played DJ. Peter drumming on the steering wheel. Peter crying in my arms telling me he was a loser and was always going to be a loser. Peter on Christmas morning wearing a Santa Claus hat and waking me up with a plate stacked with chocolate chip pancakes. Peter trapping mice and taking them to the park because he didn't believe in killing them. Peter screwing me before he went to work. Peter flicking his special Zippo I had bought him. Peter rubbing his dick and then smelling his hand, not knowing I was watching. The way he ate peanut butter out of the jar, taking a bite, smoothing it over, scraping the edges so he didn't waste any. Peter handing me the iPod he had put all my music on. Peter lying on the bed wearing briefs that were way too small for him. 'They fit me good, right?' he had asked. Peter, always smelling like soap, his clean, scrubbed skin. His perfectly clean asshole. If I had to eat off someone's asshole, his would be my first choice. Peter playing an obscure Bob Dylan song to me on our anniversary in a terrible Mexican wedding shirt. How many fucking memories were there?

'Can we please watch something else?'

Douglass said, 'C'mon. Let me finish this. We always watch what you want.'

This was the most untrue statement anyone had ever made in the universe. Douglass always had the remote. Any time I put something on, he guffawed and complained till I gave it back. Douglass left the apple core sitting on the coffee table, because the apple core fairy was going to come by and flutter away with it. It would sit there for days, just like that fucking brown bag. In order not to have a complete mental breakdown, I didn't let my brain ponder what gross rotten thing was in that brown crumpled bag. Douglass was selfish. He just thought, 'I don't fucking live here. So I'll throw shit everywhere.'

Addiction is so boring. Look at that dumb person doing the same dumb thing over and over all the time and not doing much of anything else. That's addiction. Repeating the same thing, the same cycle, the exact same thoughts.

Sit there. Look at your fucking phone. You can stop it right now. You are officially boring the fuck out of yourself. Your problems are becoming old problems.

'These are old blues,' Joanna Newsom sang.

Eventually the guy showed up. After he had put us through hell for three days, we didn't even mention it. Douglass handed him the money and went to the kitchen with the bundle. Knowing I was about to get high made my body feel high already. Someone told me about this girl who got wet as soon as she felt the dope in her hand. I heard the familiar rattling sounds of Douglass going through my spoons, even after I had asked him to reuse the same one. I smiled at the guy. He had a cute grin. Wore bright sneakers. He was always a dick on the phone and always polite in person. I rambled a little about how things were good, just to show him there were no harsh feelings. I felt weirdly embarrassed about all the texts and phone calls. He wished us a good day and slammed the door. And just like that, I knew it was going to be a good day.

Douglass came in and put the bundle on the coffee table, already ripped open. I didn't count the bags. I didn't care how many Douglass had taken from my portion. I would later, when I was down to my last two, but right then it was a bounty.

'Stay away from needles,' Douglass said as he wrapped a belt around his arm. He used his mouth to hold the sleeve of his shirt up. He put the needle in his arm. His mouth let go of the sleeve. His eyes closed. He went, 'Damn!'

Even after the sickness subsided and the sweats stopped and that warm feeling came and another movie started, I was still not okay. When you go through day after day of numbness, you forget what feelings are like.

Douglass said, 'When you're so strung out, it takes more than what you're used to to feel okay.'

'We should get clean,' I said.

Douglass nodded.

He said, 'You are still young, but I'm running out of time.'

He said, 'You can do something, or you can be a junkie. You are fooling yourself if you think you can do both.'

One of the only good things about getting high with Douglass was that he didn't nod out like most long-term users.

The real junkie nod is frustrating to watch. They slowly droop forward until they are completely bent over. They keep dropping their cigarette. You watch them light it, lean over, drop it, and then wake up and pick it up and then instantly drop it again. You watch their head fall forward until it hits the coffee table. Every time they say they are just tired. Every time they say, 'No, I'm awake,' and they light a cigarette and they slump over and they drop it. And you want to scream, 'Put out the cigarette and just lie down.' How fucking hard is that?

'Why can't he just lie down?' I asked Elizabeth the time we watched Noah do it.

'I don't know why,' she said.

Douglass told me, 'I have Tourette's. I don't know I'm doing it, so if I do it just tell me and I'll stop.'

He would hop and holler and make loud nonsense jokes and repeat himself over and over.

Sometimes you say, 'Can you please stop?'

'Please stop.'

'Stop what?'

My ass felt itchy, so I got in the shower, turned on the water, turned around, and spread my cheeks, so all the water went inside my ass. I was freezing cold. There's probably some guy out there who would be turned on by licking shit off your asshole. Whatever weird thing you can think of, there has to be some freak whose favorite thing in the world is that exact thing. When you think of everyone who has ever been born and everyone alive right now and every human that will be alive until an asteroid hits us or global warming sets off a series of natural disasters or we just ping-pong from planet to planet and leave colonies behind, out of all those people, there has to be someone who is into whatever your mind can come up with. Like some guy who jerks off by rubbing his dick on different kinds of cheese, or some guy who eats bugs as he jacks himself. Then there are the weird things everyone knows about, like men who are into amputees or handicapped women. I bet there's some guy who jerks off by rubbing his cock on books. Like his dick gets paper cuts, and he cringes in pain, but he kind of loves it more than anything in the world.

I cleaned my room. I cut up magazines and made a collage on the wall. I could do whatever I wanted. I played music, and I read a book about Chinese factory workers. I was pretty grateful I was not a Chinese factory worker. I was lazy.

I took a bubble bath and felt like a movie star.

The weeks flew by. I scoured craigslist personals and met men. I vetted them through emails and phone calls and made sure they were my particular type, older white businessmen. Here were the surprising things: they were attractive, smart, and funny, and most of the time I would have hooked up with them without getting paid. Except I needed the money.

They liked to tell me their philosophies. 'You always have to pay with a woman. You can pay in installments by taking a woman out to dinner and buying her presents and taking her to shows. Or you can find a nice young woman and just give her the money up front and know for sure you are going to get laid.'

'If I go to a bar and pretend to be interested in whatever she is saying and hook up with her and then lie to her, that's somehow more ethical by society's standards than telling you what I want up front and paying you for it.'

They all told me how much they wanted me to enjoy it too.

Among my friends, there was a gender divide when it came to turning tricks. The women were interested. Amy told me she was kind of jealous. Elizabeth said she could never do it, but she could see how it was perfect for me. My male friends thought it sounded like the worst thing ever. But girls know it's really not that big of a deal to give head or get fucked or have a guy come on your face. As a girl, you've probably been pressured into fucking at least once, and have probably pity-fucked some loser once, and over time you've done enough stuff that you really didn't feel like doing that eventually it doesn't seem like that big of a deal.

I didn't think the response from my male friends had anything to do with safety. But they knew all their ugly, nasty desires and didn't want to think of some man doing those things to me. And no matter how progressive they were, they didn't think I could actually enjoy hooking up with these guys. If I did, that only meant I was damaged somehow. They all implied I was dumb and naive, that these johns were the ones winning, and I was dumb for being happy to get paid.

I was worried that after having these experiences, sex would be boring forever. When it was plain vanilla, or when I would lie there, thinking, *I could be getting paid to do this.*

People said women who did this kind of thing had no self-respect. I had no idea what that meant, because I got off on doing it. I liked meeting these dudes and hearing their life stories. I liked being told I was hot. I liked being told what to do. It was the first time in my life I felt like I was getting paid for being me. When they handed me cash, I felt like a champ.

Sometimes I wondered if I was harming my psychological well-being by validating my inner desire to be treated like shit, but what turns you on turns you on, I figured, and if being treated like shit made me feel really fucking good, then good for me, right?

Imagine a world where people didn't have hang-ups. Where I could have gone to a job interview, and said, 'I've been hooking up with men for money, but I think I want to try working here now.' Where I could talk about it with people the same way other people talked about their jobs. It wasn't fair I had to have these secrets when I didn't feel like I was doing anything secretive.

It isn't always so straightforward. Sometimes they will say things that stick in your mind. You don't know why, but once in a while they talk to you in a certain tone and call you a whore, and you want to punch them in the face.

You meet a real estate agent at a bar on the Upper East Side. He tells you the story you've heard before, a million times over, about why he is on craigslist, 'I work all the time. I don't have time to meet anyone.' You giggle too much. You are giddy. He eyes you. You shift in your seat. He doesn't. He talks about work. He drops names, acts arrogant, shows off. You act like you can't believe how talented and rich and well connected he is. He asks about school. He asks you where you're from. You lie and say Virginia. He asks about your background. You lie and say you're half-white and half-Indian. He asks you how old you are. Twenty-five, you lie. You grow tired of answering questions.

It's easier to lie about everything. You're playing a role. They aren't falling for *you*. You're a twenty-five-year-old college kid whose boyfriend dumped her. That's your story. They all say, 'Fuck him. Believe me, you're better off this way.'

They all get off on the age thing. 'Twenty-five? That's hot.'
    'I hope I'm not too old for you.'
    'Have you ever been with an older man?'
    'No,' you answer to every single one of them, 'I've like fanta-sised about it, but I've never actually done it, so …'

'The truth is I don't really have a lot of experience with guys. Like, I've only had two boyfriends, but I was with them forever,' you say, acting as if you're embarrassed.
    'That's cool,' they smirk.

There comes a moment when you haven't registered any obvious signs of psychosis, so you just need to decide whether to go or not. Because once you enter one of those short-stay hotels, or their apartments, you will be alone with them, and they can do anything.

You giggle in a cab. *This is an adventure.* He tells you to smoke a cigarette and wait five minutes and then go into the building with the black awning and tell the man behind the counter you are here to see apartment 4C. 'You are here to look at an apartment you are considering renting,' he tells you. *This is fun.* You walk in and look around like you are considering, 'Hmm, this is a nice lobby.' The man behind the counter cradles a phone between his head and shoulder. He nods and smiles. You get in the elevator. You ask the real estate agent to give you a tour. He does. The apartment is beautiful. Stainless steel everything and granite counters. Flat-screen on the wall. Comfy couches.

'Does it come furnished?' you ask.

'Yeah, it can,' he says, as he puts his hands around your waist. He says you're pretty. You go down on him. He asks if he can come on your face. And then it's over in two minutes. He says, 'Hold on,' and hands you a tissue to clean up with. You both arrange yourselves by the mirror in the foyer. He hands you 150 bucks. You walk out together. He gives you a kiss on the check and says, 'Stay out of trouble, kid.'

You meet a banker at bar and he takes you on a train to Queens. He has you bend over and beats your ass. It fucking stings. You say, 'Thank you, Daddy.' He slaps your face. You say, 'Thank you, Daddy.' He feels your pussy and calls you a slut because you're so wet. Then he fucks you hard and it fucking hurts. It feels like his cock is banging right into your cervix. You take it for as long as you can, but it hurts too much, so you yell out the safe word, and he instantly stops. He takes a puff off his bong and then says, 'You okay? Did Daddy hurt you? Come here. You like *South Park*?' You watch *South Park,* but then you just want to get it over with. He bends you over and fucks you from behind. You are screaming. 'Never been fucked like that,' he says. Then he smacks you. Then he pulls your hair, 'What do you say?'

'Thank you, Daddy.'

You leave with 350 bucks. You feel weirdly relaxed, like just leaning back in the cab you could pass out.

The banker texts you in the cab, 'Get home okay?'

This is the part you don't understand. You understand the violent aggression. You understand why they pay you. But what is this thing about making sure you get home okay? Or when they throw in cab fare as you're leaving, or when they take you to buy a warmer coat, or when they give you old sweaters or lectures about how you are actually smart, or they ask about what you want to do with your life. Almost always, if you see a guy more than once, he will broach this subject and tell you that you can't do this forever. You tell him you know. You tell him you are in college. You tell him it's just for spending money.

You go through five hundred bucks in two days. Even though you don't spend it all on dope. Dope makes the money go faster. It just does, no matter how you cut it. You can have money or you can have dope, but you can't have both.

You are proud to tell anyone who knows what you do that it's no problem to back out if you don't like the way a guy looks, or if he rubs you the wrong way. One guy tells you he looks like De Niro and refuses to send you a picture, and you meet him at a shitty McDonald's on shitty Delancey Street, and he walks in looking like Joe Pesci in a coat that doesn't fit. You don't know how you are going to do this. You don't want to be with a fat man. He says, 'I'm not what you expected, huh?' And you both know. And then he shakes your hand and leaves.

They want you to beg to be fucked. When they allude to their aging body, you turn away. Women can get validation from each other and from men. Men can't get it anywhere. They work constantly and watch their bodies get old, and they think, *Why bother going out? I can't get laid anyway,* and so they look to meet you. And you want to tell them there is nothing wrong with them. It's like talking to a fourteen-year-old girl. They just don't believe you, no matter what you say.

The best one is Jimmy. He uses the phrase 'incredibly boring' five times in ten minutes when talking about his education, his job, and his life. You drag out of him that he created some kind of algorithm that makes wealthy people even wealthier. He asks you if you know what a hedge fund is. You say, 'Sure,' because you don't care. He takes you to a shrink's office he sublets to some woman. He is short. You stand face to face. He tells you to put your hands on his shoulders. He tells you to open your mouth, and he looks at your teeth. You think for a split second he is going to squeeze your throat. But he touches your hair and asks you to take off your top and pull up your skirt. He jerks off for a couple of minutes while you just stand there. Then you go down on him, and he finishes in your mouth.

Jimmy talks fast and makes jokes. He is meticulous about putting everything exactly the way it was before you leave the office.

'I need to erase all evidence we were ever here.'

'That's exactly what murderers do.'

After shifting the ottoman back and forth, he backs up and looks around the room, and says, 'Something is a little off.'

'Maybe it's your conscience.'

He kind of grins.

He sees you once a week. He writes you emails about how he thinks about you on your knees. You think about being on your knees, and how he gets his cock out of his pants and boxers like he's going to piss, and you take him in your mouth. You think of how he takes his tie and flings it over his shoulder and looks down at you. You look up at him and he closes his eyes and the camera zooms back, and there is a business man getting a blow job in this room.

All he ever wants is for you to wear a skirt and give him a blow job. He tells you that you are his therapy. When he kisses you, he grins and takes out his Trident gum. He is boyishly handsome. He tells you he never lets anyone take his picture because he is too self-conscious.

His cock always smells like soap.

He loves clever company names and company mottos, like the porta-potty company, 'Call A-Head.'

'Get it?' he asks. 'Like a head is a toilet ' He claps his hands and smiles. 'Love it '

Jimmy asks you if you'll just have a drink with him.

When you lie on the couch with your legs in his lap, he talks about the death of his sister. You listen, and he asks, 'I'm not wasting your time, am I?'

On the cab ride home you always feel high.

You meet a European guy at the restaurant of a fancy hotel and enjoy the best meal of your entire life. Octopus, both crispy and soft. Melted dark chocolate with hazelnuts on top spread on lightly salted, toasty bread. Real food is a shock to your system. You want to puke after having subsided only on yogurt for who knows how long. You feel all the carbs and sugar invade your veins like dope. You are buzzed and then so tired you can hardly keep your eyes open. You go up to the room and leave him to flirt with a black woman with short hair and big tits. You snort a bag and take a shower, trying to wake up. He comes in while you're in the shower. You go down on him for a few minutes, and then he leaves. You stay in the shower forever. When you come out, you two fool around. He eats you out until you pretend to have an orgasm. You have a screaming and shaking routine, and you do it. Then he says he's tired and falls asleep. The food feels heavy in your stomach, and you wish you could puke it up. You watch half an episode of *Top Chef* and then the rerun that comes on after it.

In the morning he tries to put it in your butt but you refuse, so instead he jerks off into your butt crack and then leaves five hundred bucks in cash on a dresser. He says he is in a hurry, but you can stay as long as you want to. The room is rented for another day. You put on the softest robe ever. You stuff all the toiletries into your purse.

It seems like kind of a shame to leave a beautiful hotel room, but you are out of drugs and there is nothing on TV.

When you leave you can't wipe the smirk off your face. Five hundred bucks. Five hundred.

Sometimes if you leave your fate to people, they don't disappoint you. When no one's looking and it doesn't matter, a stranger can change your whole life for a little while.

Then you have three bad dates in a row.

A sad man takes you to a shitty Indian restaurant. He is so lonely, he tells you.

You stare at his wrinkled shirt. You wonder if his wife is dead.

An asshole who yells at waiters and is abrupt starts grabbing at you and then takes you to a hotel room. When you go down on him and his dick falls out of your mouth, he smacks you, hard. He laughs. You try to laugh, trying to play it off like you're both enjoying this game. Sick weird fuck. He says he is forty-five, but he has to be pushing sixty. You stop and say you want to leave. He surprises you by paying you in full and then sharing a cab with you. He jokes around with you like you are best pals.

Then one night you go to Brooklyn. You think it's funny because for you, this is a desperate move. You imagine all these junkies at NA sharing their 'hitting rock bottom' story, and yours would be, 'I knew I wasn't myself when the train left Jay Street and plunged deeper into Brooklyn.' The date consists of talking to a British guy. He ends up walking you back to the station. By then you kind of hate him. On the way back to the apartment you talk to your mother, and she bothers you about seeing a dentist. You turn the corner down the alley toward the back entrance of your building. You feel your hair being pulled. Your mind is trying to figure out what the fuck is going on. Who could it be? You think, *This is not funny* and then you are being thrown onto the cement. As you fall you catch the eye of your assailant, a crazy-eyed young woman with a red bandana. There are two fuzzy figures behind her. You are completely vulnerable lying there on the ground. You see cash has fallen out of your purse. Your mind tries to put together what is happening. This can't be rape because it's a woman. This can't be a robbery because no one is interested in the money. They are surrounding you. In slow motion you see her big boot draw back to kick you, and you think, *This is going to hurt.* You know by the impact that this is serious. Your vision dims. You think about how in cartoons stars appear when someone is hit in the head. You wait for the pain but there isn't any. Your hearing isn't working right. You see their mouths moving. Nothing. Then the murmurs fade in and out. 'Oh shit ' you hear one of them yell. Something is wrong. The other two kick you, one in the gut, which makes you curl over, which sets you up to get kicked again in the head, and then you hear noise and register it as laughter. They run off. You stand up, and you are missing a platform shoe. Do you take off your other shoe, or do you look for the missing one? You hold one shoe and your bag, and they didn't even take the fucking cash so you have to pick it up. Your phone is probably fucked, and the battery is lying on the concrete. Now the pain hits you. Your stomach feels like it's bleeding. Your hand touches a swelling eyelid. Now the fear hits you; they could come back. You can't stop shaking. They could come back. You have never felt so vulnerable. Blood pours out of your knee where the stocking has ripped. You make it to the back gate, about ten feet from where you were attacked, and you call 'help' through the gate, but there is no one around. It can't be past 9:00 p.m. Where are the dog walkers and the parents with their kids coming back from the grocery store or play dates? You are shaking, but you manage to put the battery back in your phone. You thank fucking Christ as the word 'Sprint' swirls around. Douglass picks up after one ring. Once inside, you try to lie down and discover you can't. Douglass wants to go out and look for them. 'They ran,' you tell him, hoping he will stop being a dude, put away his figurative cock that wants to protect you, and just be comforting instead.

Your vision is snowy, like the reception is all fucked-up. You touch the back of your head. The blood is cartoon red.

Douglass watched the news. 'It's that knockout game. From the back you were wearing all black, so they thought you were Jewish. These young, stupid teenagers, mostly black kids, hit Jewish people in the head.'

'Shit, that's why they ran when they saw my face.' The fact did not bring any of the relief I would have expected. It only made me think, *If I were Jewish, would I be dead? What would they do to an actual Jewish person?* This then led to an uncomfortable quandary. 'Should we call the police?'

'I don't know.'

I slept for the next two days, awakening only to snort a few lines. My stomach hurt. It felt like my ribs were broken, but if they truly were, I probably wouldn't have been able to stand it. The hardest thing to deal with was how ugly and stupid people could be. My attackers were sadistic and cruel. I wasn't a real person to them, but like an extra in *Grand Theft Auto*. All I could do was lie there. Sometimes I thought about taking a shower, but sitting up was a nightmare.

'You're so lucky you're a writer,' Elizabeth said as she lifted up a part of the floor. Like a piece of the fucking floor. One of the wood planks was cut in half, and she lifted it up. She pulled out a dusty antique box and started going through the stuff in it, putting the occasional empty bag to the side.

'I haven't written in forever,' I said. 'I don't even think of myself as a writer.' I was thinking, *How did she do that? Could I just make a hole in my floor? That was so cool.*

'But you can write, you have a place where you can put everything. I don't know where to put things. You can make something out of all the ugliness.' She looked up at me. She had tears in her eyes. 'What am I supposed to do with all the shit that happens to me?'

There isn't much you could maintain when you have to worry about scoring every day so you don't get sick. My life was a waiting room, a TV room, and then back to a waiting room.

When you're around other junkies, no one speaks while everyone is waiting. Come back after the dope arrives and no one can stop talking and laughing. Everyone talks excitedly about their plans, and no one talks about how addicted we all know we've become.

You could turn to another junkie, and say, 'I really need to stop.' And you will be met with a knowing nod and the words, 'Yeah, me too.' Everyone always says it. Everyone probably means it.

Only one of my johns knew about my drug use. He talked to me about NA, and once when I snorted a bag in front of him, he said, 'C'mon. Please don't do that. I don't want to take your ass to the hospital.'

There were no track marks to hide.

I got cash from dudes and then gave my cash to dudes who sold me drugs.

I wanted regulars. Every time I saw a guy, he talked about seeing me again, but I got used to not hearing back from them. I got used to never believing anyone. They wanted variety. That's why they contacted me to begin with.

Also, I wasn't thin and blonde. I could have cleaned up if I was.

Men hate when you talk about your body. This guy Kevin said, 'Shut up. I don't care at all.'

The more money they had, and the more money they gave me, the nicer and more respectful they were.

My days continued: getting high, either going out for a date or not, either getting more drugs or not. Sometimes I read.

Sometimes it felt like there was blackness underneath everything. Like a Rothko painting, how the blackness bleeds through. Feeling everything led to nothing, and there was nothing I could do about it. Day after day of being alone and numb and fucking strangers and having cash and blowing it all, and then knowing in a day or so I'd have plenty more. It would just go on like that till my teeth fell out, till I didn't even have the strength to pull myself out of it. No kids, no family, me alone except for the growing terror my dreams weren't in the future but somewhere far behind me. I had to figure something out, because I knew this couldn't last forever – but whatever, if

I didn't get a bag today then it would be fucking horrible, so get me another bag. I needed a break just from thinking about it.

One more day, and then I'll stop. Wait, I should taper down a little. Wait, I need to get Xanax first. Wait, I have a date in two days, so why shouldn't I use a little longer to make a lot more money? Always thinking, *One last big score.* Go out with a bang.

Douglass kept running out and getting dope, and I always had the money but it couldn't all maintain.

—

I didn't mean to kill myself, but nobody believes me. I did a lot of dope, but not more than I'd ever done before. Maybe it was the Xanax on top of the dope and the not eating or sleeping. I never would have thought Douglass would call 911 on me, so I must have scared him.

I come to vomiting white shit on the floor of the living room. Then the ambulance shows up, and I try to tell everyone really I'm okay, but once I'm in the ambulance the EMT leans in and says, 'My advice to you is if you really want to get home, act normal.' She says this with an air of confidentiality, like she is relaying a secret code. I take the advice to heart and go with it.

I fool the doctor. He asks me about the nasty black shit they make me drink that has the consistency of paint, and I joke about why they don't sell it in vending machines. I think, *What would a person who isn't suicidal do in this situation?* Obviously, a normal person would go crazy, asking questions about why they couldn't go home, but so would someone trying to get home to off themselves, so playing 'normal' means I'm not even freaked out because I know I didn't do anything wrong, and so I'm just going to be chill and joke around. It's the fat, annoying nurse who sees through me. 'What happened? So were you trying to hurt yourself?'

I don't know how the laws work, but I'm pretty sure the doctor isn't going to call the cops if I tell him I do dope. But I don't. I tell him I have anxiety attacks and took more Xanax than I should have, and also I drank some wine. I don't know if they will test me and figure out the truth. The nurse looks at me like she doesn't believe a word I'm saying.

The nurse is a short-haired, bitchy cunt. How could you work in health and be on your feet all day and still be that fat? How much does this woman eat?

The nurse seems suspicious, and I'm pretty sure even if it was an accident she would still be suspicious. She knows there's more to the story.

I overhear the doctor and the nurse discussing me. The doctor sounds pretty sure it was an accident. The nurse is adamant it wasn't. The doctor compromises; they will put me on a normal ward (instead of the loony bin) but keep me for observation.

This is not good for a number of reasons. The most immediate one is I am starting to get dope sick. Maybe it's just knowing

I will be dope sick, since it hasn't been that long since I used. But it will happen, and the anxiety makes me feel queasy and desperate. Douglass needs to get in a cab and go back home and get my shit and then bring it back before they move me to a room. I can't find my phone. I don't want to appear too anxious. When I ask about it, the nurse says I'll get a phone once a bed opens up. When will that be? She doesn't know. Can I just have my phone back? She says she'll try. She won't try.

Hospitals are full of people trying to help people. There is not one person who can help you.

Can I just walk out? I decide to give it a shot. But then the curtain opens, and they are taking my blood.

'I have to pee.'

'This will only take a second.' The woman is already putting the rubber thing around my arm, pinching the fuck out of my skin when she twists it.

'Fuck.'

I normally look away, but this time I look right at the horror-movie-huge needle as it spikes into my vein. I sneeze. And then sneeze again. She tells me to sit still. I can't. I am in the middle of a hospital and am sick and nobody can help me.

When she's gone, I leave. I walk past the dying people. Wives and husbands. A smattering of lonely, old people. There is a gay couple. The dude looks like a poster for AIDS. Weird how AIDS seems kind of retro now – even diseases have a golden age, a prime, and then they seem played out. How annoying to get AIDS now, feeling like a song people remember being on the radio a lot but have since forgotten completely. His lover is holding his hand and whispering to him. All the other waiting people sit around like they've done this a million times before. I found my clothes under my bed so the plan is to transform from patient to visitor.

I don't get far. I stick to my story of how I'm feeling fine now, and so I wanted to go out just for a smoke, but the nurse goes and tattles on me to the doctor, and he is not entirely positive I wasn't trying to flee.

Over the following days I undergo a horrible nasty withdrawal in the hospital. But finally they get ahold of my shrink, who tells them I need to be on Suboxone. At last, some relief. I sleep. The shrink also okays clonazepam, and they are generous with it. Then there's talk about where I'm going to go. My mother and Raj are there. I don't know when they came. I don't even know what the conversation is. I'm too out of it to stay awake longer than forty-five minutes. There is a twenty-four-hour period where I am almost asleep the entire time. Then there is a twenty-four-hour period where I can't sleep at all, and I have no visitors. I try to watch the television, but it's only loud enough to be annoying.

I can't focus but feel alert. The nightmare withdrawal symptoms are pretty much behind me. It's plausible I could be clean. I call my mother. She doesn't believe me. She says she's tired and doesn't know what to do. I get angry. She thinks it's reasonable I tried to kill myself, or at least stupidly OD'd. 'I know you were taking …' She doesn't finish the sentence. Like there's a word that can't be spoken aloud. She won't say it. Which is weird, because she always has something to say.

I end up on a plane with my mother and brother. I keep thinking, *Sound normal.* But I can tell by the worry on their faces that I've scared the shit out of them. My mother tries to figure out where I'm getting the dope. She doesn't know Douglass has been staying with me. Thank god he was gone when they went back to the apartment before I was discharged.

There are thirty-four texts. Johns. Money.

It is so hard to know money is waiting for you, a lot of money, and every single problem you currently have – feeling like shit, wanting to die, guilt, anger, resentment, feeling soft, feeling vulnerable – could all disappear easily, and you really would be completely fine. You try to stick with this thought process but you know eventually you will feel this way again. You will be in this same exact position only more time will have passed, and so it's better just to clean up now.

A small voice says, 'You won't ever get high again?'

Another voice says, 'No, one day. Like in six months, it will be okay to do a few bags and your tolerance will be so shitty you will feel incredible.'

And then another voice says, 'It's time. Just fucking stop it. You are too old for this to be cute.' I try to hold on to that. I am a former drug addict. Oh god, that sounds terrible.

I'm actually clean. The Suboxone is helping me along.

The place they put me in is like a prison with carpeting. There is a door you have to punch a code into to leave.

I scream at my mother, 'How can you fucking leave me here?' She just cries. She says she doesn't know what to do anymore. 'So you just fucking lock me up? I have rights.' I didn't know that my shrink and my mother had conspired when I was in the hospital in New York.

Here, kid, this is what you did with the life that was given to you.

I cry a lot. I think about how Peter would have visited if we were still together. My mother annoys me with her questions, and my brother is eager to get back home. He's annoyed I do whatever I want, and he has to take time out of his life to deal with my shit. Like I had asked him to come. 'Here, deal with my shit.'

Glad-Ass, the head of the useless nurses, says my roommate will be in soon. I ask if she can leave me alone for a while, but she says I'm on twenty-four-hour watch. She follows me to the bathroom and looks directly at me when I pull down my pants and go. She takes me to the rec room, which is just one big room with a couch and a big table, the kind they have at preschools, and a TV and a Ping-Pong table. The whole place feels like an after-school recreation center.

My roommate's name is Keisha. She's twenty-five years old but looks almost forty. She's fat and wears a scarf over her head and sucks on a lollipop.

Keisha's mom is on crack. I know this because Keisha said, 'My mom is on crack.'

I can no longer cry. The drugs must be working.

Keisha says this place is all right, better than a lot of other places. I tell her I like her beaded bracelet around her ankle, and she says she'd make me one.

I lie there in the dark. If sleep ever happened to me again, it would feel like a small miracle. Keisha is snoring. I prop my leg up against the wall and run my hand through the bars of light that fall on the wall. I wonder how long I'll be here, and then my body starts itching inside for a cigarette. I grind my teeth and turn over a couple times, feeling like I want to beat the shit out of somebody. There are places where they let you smoke, but this is not one of those places. I get up and walk over to the nurse's station and say I can't sleep. The woman behind the counter has a fat, friendly face – like a waitress in a diner who you think probably spends all her time in the back eating banana splits – and she gives me two pills, and I swallow them without asking what they are.

I lie in bed and start to cry again. Where the fuck is bottom? Is this finally it? I miss Peter's sleeping body. My head is a dusty room cluttered with sad, broken things from another time. I remember our first year, when I would make dinner for him like a good wife. When I would rush around making sure the apartment was clean, and he would come home tired and shitty. He would kiss me on the cheek and stuff his face and tell me how great dinner was.

Does Peter know I am in here? Do I even want him to? Would he think, *Of course, she's in the loony bin. Of course, I'm glad I'm not with her anymore.* He is out there in the world having fun. He is out there in the world, and whatever he does is no longer my business.

I miss being someone's wife. I am divorced, a failure, a reject. Someone had picked me and then thought, *Whoops, this isn't the one I wanted.* I had been given a million chances, and I was cavalier with all of them.

If you're the woman, you're the one who everyone pities. The one everyone secretly thinks is the failure.

When I wake up, I open the drawers and find all my stuff is gone. I look for my shoes that were right next to the door, and they're gone too, so I walk up to the nurses' station. Glad-Ass won't talk to me till I'm on the other side of a fat white piece of tape. I get behind the tape and tell her all my stuff is gone. And she tells me, in this tone like she's already said it at least a million times, I'll get my stuff back when I earn it. I tell her I don't understand. She says you get points for following rules; little by little, I'll get all my stuff back. I nod, thinking, *These people are fucking nuts.*

They treat you like you are five years old. You are being told what to do by people who are obviously stupid.

Doesn't being here confirm what I always knew deep down? What everyone always knew? I am batshit crazy.

There's a point system. You get points for finishing your food. You get points for participating in therapy. You get points for making art in art therapy. When you get a certain amount of points you get to make a phone call. When you get a certain amount of points you get to check out certain things from your own stuff to use during free time.

The windows are tinted, and it always looks grey outside.

In the mornings they fill us with sugar. Three fluffy brown pancakes we drown in syrup and slather with globs of butter, falling apart all hot in my mouth. Then we drink thick whole milk that clings to my belly like cream. Then there are glazed donuts and Lucky Charms and Frosted Flakes. I eat two of the pancakes, but soon my stomach feels like it's sticking together, with the milk holding it down like lead. Keisha stacks her pancakes and makes sure they are lined up perfectly around the edges. I watch the little hairs, all sticky and shiny, on her pretty lip.

We're not allowed to have razors, or anything with caffeine, or candy, drugs, or gum. If we are caught with any of these things we will be punished.

All the girls' legs are so hairy. I touch the fur on my own and wonder how thick it's going to get, and how nice it's going to be when I finally get to shave it, watching the long, soft hairs fall away and leading the razor up, making a path through the forest of hair.

This place is for teaching you about structure. Everyone knows structure helps.

You get used to the routine. You yawn ten minutes before lights out. You wake up ten minutes before the nurse comes in to wake you up. Your stomach growls right before the lunch tray comes.

You hardly ever see your shrink, a fresh-faced young guy with black hair and retro eyeglasses. He is supposed to check in with you once a day, but it's more like every two or three days. You wonder what his cock is like. You have been with enough men to know that no matter what someone looks like, they are capable of being a total freak. He is intelligent. You can tell by the eyes. How some people, like the nurses, have eyes that are dull, just dull and glazed over, like nothing is happening behind them. But the shrink's eyes are contemplative. You wonder what it might feel like to get on your knees and unzip his pants, to feel his hand resting on your head as you take him in your mouth. How he would sigh. You miss making people feel good. Time is so slow. It hasn't been that long. It feels like forever. It's been nine days.

You tell him how you were married once and had your shit together. You tell him all you have to do is finish your thesis and then you will have a master's and maybe could teach. You tell him you've been keeping a journal. You tell him the divorce was for the best. You don't know why you keep lying. Sometimes you tell him you're a liar, but he never questions what you say.

When your mother visits you just end up fighting. You try and fail to explain, without screaming, how awful this place is. She says it's good for you to be here. You tell her she has no idea what the fuck she's talking about. This place is not good for anyone. She's never known what was good for you because she doesn't know you. She has an imaginary daughter she has mistaken you for. How could you be someone you aren't? She cries, and you feel horrible.

That is the only time she visits. Over the phone, she tells you it's difficult finding someone to drive her. You ask her why she brought you to DC if she wasn't going to visit. If you were in New York then at least your friends could have visited. You tell her this is all bullshit anyway; you weren't even trying to hurt yourself. 'I take a few extra Xanaxes because I can't sleep, and you lock me in a fucking nut house!'

'I'm doing the best I can!'

'Yeah, and my husband divorces me. Did you ever think of

coming and staying with me like a normal mother would have instead of telling me to get over it? You don't understand what it's like. You don't just get over something like that!'

'There were needles in that apartment. You think I'm an idiot! You think I don't know you had that guy staying there?'

You hang up the phone because you don't know what to say.

You wake up feeling shitty and take your meds and take a piss with the door open. Some of the nurses turn their heads, but some of them look right at you. You don't care if they look anymore. Then you go to morning meeting. The nurse asks to speak to you privately.

'You need to wear a bra.'

'Why? There are only women here.'

'It's part of the rules to dress appropriately.'

'But what difference does it make?'

'You're refusing to comply with the rules,' she says, looking down at a clipboard.

'No. Jesus, I'm just trying to figure out what the point is.'

'Go back to your room and put on a bra, or you're not getting any points for the day.'

You want to say, 'Go ahead.' But you've learned it's not worth it. You know when you're beat. And in this place you're always going to be the loser. The nurse gets to go home and drink coffee and read books however she wants to. She has a life that is progressing. She gets to be outside. She gets to eat when she feels like eating, sleep when she feels like sleeping. Your life is on pause.

The meds must be doing their magic because you don't feel emotions that strongly. You don't cry every night. You stop getting so angry. Thoughts come and register but nothing overwhelms you. There is this weird optimism, and you have no idea what is generating it or where it comes from. It must be the Prozac – a little pill that makes you feel stupidly happy about absolutely nothing.

You spend all of the free time one morning writing a letter to Ogden. You tell him everything. It's kind of nice to write something longhand. You brought a laptop but aren't allowed to touch it because it has a camera. They don't want anyone's privacy to be violated. They don't give you your books because you're supposed to engage with people.

If you ever had any hope that this might not be a total waste of time, you don't anymore.

There is a young woman who attacked her mother with a knife. There is a woman who lost her kid to cancer and never talks. She's obviously in some kind of shock. There is a girl who thinks you're the funniest person in the ward. She's pretty dumb.

Sometimes it feels like you are being punished, and the *real* program is to make you so miserable that you don't try to use or off yourself again, because you may fail and have to come back.

That's pretty much the lesson you take away: next time kill yourself properly, or don't try.

You have group therapy sessions every morning. You have to go around the room and say how you feel. You can't say, 'Fine.' 'Fine' is not a feeling word. They have a chart with feeling words beneath faces expressing the feeling. Scan the chart. Anxious? Optimistic? Enraged? Excited? What is there to be excited about in a place where each day is exactly the same? They probably increase your meds if you say that.

Sometimes you cry and beg the nurses to let you go out and take a walk. Will you please just take me for a walk?

You see people freak the fuck out. One time someone screams at you. Not words. A black girl with hair so short she doesn't look like a girl stands right in front of you and screams her head off, and you stand there staring, wondering what to do. She could kill you. But then the men in white come and take her away. It doesn't seem right to lock a human up for being sick, but you can no longer muster a sense of outrage.

There is an attractive man who comes with a woman wearing unflattering clothes; they tell us to write poetry. You plagiarise a Counting Crows song and everyone is impressed.

There is a lot of therapy: group therapy, art therapy, writing therapy, the dreaded music therapy. Some people get into that shit. Some people paint with a fury, or draw maniacally and with great concentration. For a solid hour this one girl takes a piece of white paper and makes it dark black. She uses black crayons and writes with a little-kid scrawl, over and over, and when she finishes she looks somewhat satisfied, and then she picks up another piece of white paper.

I earn enough points to check out the collected works of Robert Lowell. 'I am a thorazined fixture / in the immovable square-cushioned chairs / we preoccupy for seconds like migrant birds.'

I call Ogden from the pay phone, but he doesn't pick up. He never picks up. I would bet money he was staring at the number and hitting 'Ignore.' I would ignore me too. In the message I try to sound just broken enough for him to care, but also together enough so he isn't scared I will go batshit crazy on him.

On visiting day everyone has visitors but me. It's not like I wanted to see my mother, but not having visitors is annoying. Just sitting there trying to read while overhearing parents trying to force small talk. Keisha's cousins have bright sneakers and sneak in food: candy and chicken and soda. The nurses never come in during visiting hours.

Ogden calls. He tells me he's glad I'm getting help. He says he knows it must suck. He says he's proud of me. He gives me some perspective. This is only a stop. Life will go on. I ask him if he misses me, and he says, 'Sure.' I can tell he wants to get off the phone. It always feels like there is this meter ticking that runs out before I'm done telling him what I want.

When I get off the phone, I feel sadder than I did before I spoke to him. I looked forward to things like phone calls, and now the call came and went and it wasn't much of anything. I try to call him back but it goes straight to voicemail. Seven minutes is the exact amount of Ogden's time he will allow you to waste with your bullshit.

He approached friendship like it was something to check off the list. Call Maya in the loony bin. Take out the garbage.

Some of these broken women talk in whispers about changing their lives. Some of them act all tough and defiant. They are young, and I want to tell them there is no one they are rebelling against.

Keisha writes like a school kid. She is trying to write a letter to a judge to get her daughter back. I sit down at her desk and take out a piece of paper. Her daughter was taken away when someone called Child Protective Services came when Keisha's boyfriend was slinging weed out of their apartment, but he's gone now. Keisha tells me she's been clean and sober for five years. She couldn't take living without her kid, though, so one night she got in a fight with her mother and threw a bottle and then used the shards to slice her arm open. I can't imagine her doing this. She seems like the type to eat and lie around on the couch, like she lies around in bed here, just looking at magazines. They get on her for not showering, but she says she likes baths.

I've never seen her cry. I've seen everyone else cry. I have heard her laugh. She has a great laugh.

I offer to write the letter for her. I spend days on it. I write it and revise it a million times. It feels good to be useful.

Give me new problems. I'm tired of the same old problems.

Why can't someone interest me in my own life?

She tells me I wrote an awesome letter. It makes me feel good to see her smile and look like she has something to be excited about. I wish I could do more. She shows me pictures of a little girl with ribbons in her hair. This, she tells me, is the only reason she has for living.

Keisha and I stay up in the dark. She tells me about how her uncle had molested her. I feel like I can help her. I talk to her about getting her GED. I say I can tutor her.

There is liberation in being in a loony bin. There isn't anything else to fear. Hello, bottom, nice to meet you. Sometimes it feels exactly right. When there is a tray of food in front of me, I eat it. I wear boring, clean clothes. I listen more than I talk. I let the structure lead me through the day. I don't use my brain. I don't focus on my emotions. I am a blank slate. Everything begins here. And if I get to read a book, it will be a good day. To be able to lie in bed with my bare feet swaying.

I don't want the nurses and the doctors to know, but in my head I begin to make plans. I want to go back to school. I want to do everything exactly right. It isn't fear of coming back here so much as I don't want my life to stop again. No more time-outs.

At night I get used to screams the same as I got used to sirens in the city; the noise registers but fails to alarm anymore.

I no longer feel that crazy sense of empathy every time I hear the metal door to the quiet room close, primarily because I've witnessed enough insane temper tantrums that made me want to throw people in there myself. How hard is it to shut the fuck up while people are trying to sleep?

At least I did dope. At least I left everyone alone. At least I was quiet when I was doing my dying.

Sometimes a tiny little scream rises inside me, and I muffle it with a pillow. I tell myself I have to be the sane one in here. I have to fold my clothes. I have to shower every morning. I have to put all my books in alphabetical order, be steady, and act like all of this is very much beneath me. No, I am not crazy. My secret fantasy is not about the day I can have my own fucking bathroom where I cut up my arms as much as want.

The woman who lost her son. I have to act like she doesn't have all the reason in the world to be fucking nuts.

After three weeks, they let me go home for a weekend.

My aunt and my mother pick me up. My aunt says, 'Look at you. You've lost weight since I've seen you. You look like a boy.'

I just shake my head. Then she grabs my wrist and says, 'What did you do?' Her face changes from a smirk to a nasty look of disapproval. 'You know your mother cried?' She doesn't seem to care about the nurse sitting right across from us, who looks up as my aunt's voice rises. I understand the way people view this: me fucking with my mom.

The weekend consists of going to different relatives' houses, eating a lot of food, and lying about all the positive things I'm excited about. I talk about finishing my thesis. I talk about getting my PhD. Everybody is so encouraging; I almost kind of start believing in this future too. Nobody brings up Peter. Do they think it's not a big deal, or is it because they think it's too big a deal?

Back on the ward, they finally tell me that in a week, I'll be released. I don't feel like I'm ready.

I'm not sure why they are releasing me. It's been almost two months. I stopped trying to get points long ago. I feel comfortable in the routine. I no longer lie in bed wide-awake all night crying. I have stopped thinking of ways to torture my mother forever for putting me in a psychiatric ward. Each morning I look forward to breakfast and then breeze through group therapy (which is more like taking attendance in elementary school then actual therapy), sometimes offering a story from my childhood but mostly letting other people talk. I tried and failed to start a journal, but I enjoy reading again and love the hour before dinner. The nurses are no longer evil bitches controlling my life; they're part of the background, daily annoyances I've learned to put up with. I have started hating the patients who won't fall in line. I look at them in the same way I remember other patients had looked at me, like, 'It isn't that hard. Just shut up, and do what you're told.'

What would life on the outside be like? Fear. Dread. I've been a mouse in a cage. A girl taking a time-out. I don't trust myself. The world and the men and the drugs. The way the whole day would be free, not broken up into mindless activities for me to navigate. I could start out slowly: doing my laundry, keeping my room clean, writing at night, making myself part of the world again. I would look back at this as the nasty ending to a bad patch. I would make myself breakfast. I would make my bed. I would talk to my mother daily. I would go to job interviews. I would spend a few hours a day working on my thesis at the coffee shop. I would be one of those women at the coffee shop, sipping a coffee, laptop open, looking serious and productive. I would take meds every day that would keep me steady, and have a quiet, simple life. Or I wouldn't. I would get out and just fuck everything up again. I run my hand against the wall. Keisha laughs at something in a magazine. The bed suddenly feels comfortable, and I curl up in a fetal position. Dear world, I'm sorry, but I don't know if I will ever be the kind of person who can live with you.

—

Back in the city, I listen to Lou Reed. I write, drink tons of coffee. I stay up all night because I don't need sleep, don't need food. All the weight I put on at the nut house has fallen off me. Not long after I came back, I got lonely, and now Elizabeth's friend

Val stays at my place. He gave me two hundred bucks. He said he would give me a hundred a week but is full of excuses and barely pays me. But he does clean and that's nice.

After a while I stop taking my antidepressants because they make it so I can't come. What's more depressing than that?

My mind races. My body is shrinking. I walk to the train. Hear the *National Geographic* narrator, 'Human beings do not procreate as much as other species, but their ability to use tools and adapt to their environment, coupled with their long lives, make them one of the worst types of existing infestations. It's nearly impossible to get rid of them. Look at this one here; he's made a nest out of a bench other humans have made for sitting. Look at this one mama human with her two little chicks, all clothed in the feathers of dead birds to keep cool during the winter months. Humans have a slight fur covering their entire bodies, long silky hair on the top of their heads and around their pubis. They sustain themselves on animal protein from the farms they house to grow and breed their prey.'

Mania is fucking amazing. I talk forever.

I go on craigslist to get another date.

The john dresses like a hipster and claims to be a musician. He's cool. Maybe in his forties. I am three hours late, and he doesn't even care. 'I had to see how that movie *Flight* ended,' I explain. He laughs. We go walk around. As a way of checking him out, I had suggested getting something to eat. He says there's a twenty-four-hour diner nearby, but I feel good about him, so we go back to his place. It's the first apartment in the city I've been to with wall-to-wall carpeting.

'I feel like we're in a hotel somewhere in the Midwest.'

'Ouch', he says, pouring a glass of wine.

'Oh my god.'

'What?'

'We have the same towels', I realise that I come off way too excited about this.

'Target?'

'Yup.'

He sits down next to me, and we talk forever. We talk about how BBC shows are better than American TV. We talk about how in England they don't feel the need for every character to look like a model; the actors there look like real people. We talk about how he's never been married or lived with anyone. He talks about how unfair it would be to have a girlfriend when he's always on the road. We talk about moving all the time and being an army brat. I like him. It feels easy.

Is it awful or not that a dude who pays me for sex is easier and more enjoyable than any date I've been on?

I'm getting sweaty, and I start feeling a little sick. I had done two bags in a hurry before I left home, and I can't tell if it was not enough or too much. Now I'm drinking wine on top of it. Careful, this is how people OD.

I let the conversation lull. I should get the sex over with soon. It feels like that fairy tale where the girl turns into a pumpkin at midnight. I can tell I only have a few hours before I will need more dope or be sick. I put my hand on his leg. He said, 'We don't have to rush it.'

I can tell he is lonely. I never get lonely when I'm using drugs. Obviously he wants someone to talk to, and it makes me feel bad that he is paying me to have a conversation with him. I kind of fall in love with how pathetic and sad and human that is.

I let a few moments pass before I kiss him.

I tell him how nervous I am because I've never done this before. How I had been scared of him being a nut. He says, 'Well, I still could be.'

Will I be able to tell when a real sicko wanders into my life? Will I end up chained to a pole and raped over and over for, like, ten years? Will I end up on Oprah? Find God? Will I write a book about my experiences? I would definitely write a book if I lived though something like that. I'm actually interesting, and then I would have a story people would love to feel sick reading. Most people who are abducted or survive some harrowing, life-threatening experience are pretty boring, but everyone calls them heroes. Would it be heroic to save yourself if it was your own fault for being in that bad situation in the first place? Like, what options do you have, other than to try and not die? And if you do die, does that make you a loser instead of a hero?

For example, Lucy Grealy. Lucy Grealy had a deadly cancer as a kid and had to have her chin removed. After surviving the cancer and numerous painful reconstructive surgeries, she attended the best writing program in the country. Her book got great reviews. She lived in New York City. She was talented, young, and on the brink of mainstream success. Then she overdosed on dope. It was such a waste, I remember thinking as I read the news of her death. It was like she had beaten these extraordinary and unlikely odds, survived disfiguring cancer, and all for what? To throw out a life that had been such an ordeal to live through? How could she take life for granted when she had experienced how much suffering just being alive could entail? She had made it, in my eyes. Why did she have to be vulnerable to the same emotional suffering as everyone else? Was I mad at her for not providing me with a happy ending? Maybe the only thing suffering teaches is that suffering sucks.

My john listens intently. He says he understands what I mean, but who was I to know what her life had been like? Plus, she probably got addicted to dope from the years of being prescribed opiates after all those painful surgeries.

'I don't know why I'm talking about this. It's so depressing. I'm sorry.'

He laughs. 'No, I like talking to you.'

Maybe this guy could be the love of my life. Maybe we'd end up together.

'I'm just nervous. I've never done this before,' I lie.

I can tell he gets off on the idea of me being nervous. He says, 'You must be so nervous,' as his hand goes under my skirt. I spread my legs so he could rub my pussy. 'It's okay. It's all going to be okay, honey.' He tells me I'm a good girl. Then he finger-bangs the shit out of me. And it fucking hurts. He should cut his nails. I moan, wondering how long I have to wait to fake having an orgasm.

He takes me by the hair and stands me in front of a mirrored closet. 'I want you to watch yourself.'

There are trends in porn that become trends men want to try, or maybe it works the other way around. Like how every dude wants to come on your face; like, that probably wasn't something dudes thought to do back in the 1700s. Or maybe it was. Anyway, gagging porn is popular, and now it seems like every guy wants it. He wants to hear me gag. He pulls my hair in a ponytail and forcefully fucks my mouth. I gag and gag and then spit all the mucous onto his cock. Then he smacks my ass and says, gently, 'Is that okay? Tell me if it's not and I'll stop, okay?' I say okay. He needs my permission for a slap on the butt but didn't have qualms about being rough with my throat?

After making me gag for a while, he moves me to the couch. He goes hands free, letting me find my own rhythm.

As I'm sucking him off, my mind wanders. I think of how awful it was going to be walking by the train station so late. I wonder if he would let me crash there. But I need dope. Once I was high, what would I feel like eating? Nothing would be open. My jaw hurts. The 'job' in blow job. I wonder what would happen if I just stopped. What if I bit his cock? Would he hit me? Would he grab his cock and scream, 'What did you do?' Would he demand I leave? Would he call me a crazy bitch?

What if I start to cry and tell a story about being molested by my uncle? Keisha's story was she had been seven when it started. This guy has to pay me if I cry.

Finally, he lets out a sigh. 'I'm going to come,' he says. Thank god. I don't want to swallow it, but once it's in my mouth it seems weird to spit it out. So I swallow it. It tastes so gross it makes me instantly gag. When I sit up, he kisses me softly and puts his arm around me. I kind of wish he was my man. Maybe he would be. Maybe this was the way we came into each other's lives.

I ask him if he's vegetarian.
    'Yes, why?'
    'Your come. Vegetarian come is the worst. So bitter.'
    'Huh,' he says.
    Now he probably thinks I suck cocks all the time if I can so readily link a man's diet to his come.

He calls me a freak, so I call him a freak and he laughs. He has on boxers and a wifebeater. I'm fully dressed. I don't feel sick at all. I don't want to leave. I want him to ask me to stay. I want to cuddle. I want to wake up in his arms. I want him to nurse me off dope and to never have to go home again.

He points at the white envelope on the coffee table, then gets up and hands it to me. 'Here you go, hun. Make sure you get home safe. Text me when you get home, okay?' I hope he doesn't notice how sad I am that he wants me to go. I tell him he can call me again. He nods like he will, but he probably won't. I am so tired of people, and how they get you to like them and then make it so hard to be close to them. He's the one who wanted to talk for hours. I was prepared to just get on with it and go, but he needed me to like him. He needed to be close to someone. His sink has one cereal bowl in it. I linger a little too long, but he doesn't change his mind. We hug and kiss like we care about each other. I know he just kisses me because he doesn't want to be rude. He throws on a black T-shirt with the logo for some band he'll never play for me.

On the way home, I think about the moment I had a line of spit drooling from my mouth after gagging on him when he thrust too much and too hard, and he wiped the spit from my lips and said, 'Look at what a mess you made.'

I email him when I get to my apartment. *If you want to see me again, I'm down for it.*

Three quick bags of dope get me so high I'm sick. I nod at the computer. I feel fucking great. Tomorrow or the next day I am going to get clean. I feel prepared for it, mentally.

I go to a group job interview at Urban Outfitters. The interviewer asks what we would do if a coworker was stealing.

Everyone gets really cheesy about how stealing makes everyone look bad. I tell a story about an old coworker who changed the price of a pile of books to ninety-nine cents apiece, when in fact the store didn't sell any books for ninety-nine cents. I don't get the job.

I am doing about six or seven bags a day. That's sixty or seventy bucks a day, but then I also am paying for Val's shit. I am supporting both of our drug addictions by turning tricks. God, it sounds so much worse than it feels.

I can make two or three hundred bucks a day hanging out with these dudes, or $7.50 an hour.

My biggest fear is they'll look at me and think, *Oh, god, she's not that hot.*

Only one time did I meet a guy who was a jerk. He took me to the movies. He talked dirty. We fooled around in the theater, and then he said, 'I'll be right back. I have to go to the bathroom.' He was gone for a while, so I went outside. That's when I saw his text: 'I'm sorry but I had to leave. I can't pay you when I wouldn't do you for free.' I knew what had happened. He had gotten off in the bathroom. Instead of just screwing me out of my money, he had to make me feel like shit too.

I see Jimmy the next day. We meet at the Time Warner Center. I am running late. I am always running late. I give him a hug.

Once inside, we make out. I'm not into kissing, but I don't know what to do with him. He isn't naturally dominant. It's so much easier when they tell me what to do. Like with the banker: just do as you're told, and then it's over and you get paid. I kind of hate when it's up to me, but I like that he's gentle.

He tells me I'm pretty.

Afterwards, he says, 'You know there's no other way in the world two people like us would be in the same room together.'

I see this advertising executive who wants head at the office. I can't believe how fucking cool his office is. The guy is bald. He is funny, easy to talk to. He likes big girls, so I don't feel self-conscious about my body. He comes in like five minutes. He gives me 150 bucks. Afterwards, I tell him how badly I want to work in advertising. He tells me this has been his whole life. I am sick with envy. I want him to help me. This won't work if I'm not clean. I have a reason now. I have something to not fuck up. I have something I don't want to regret.

When I get home I think about it and text him. I say I'll give him head, but instead of money maybe he can help me and give me advice. He doesn't respond.

—

'Ogden, I can't seem to stay clean.'

    'Jesus, Maya. I thought you straightened up at the psych ward. What happened?'

'I don't know. I'm doing less. I'm on this cycle where I clean up, get money, and then I think I'll do it once and then three weeks go by.'

'Have you thought of going to meetings?'

'Meetings?'

'It really helped my girlfriend when –'

'Did you say girlfriend? How old is she? What does she do? I thought we agreed you were going to spend the rest of your life celibate, punctuated by nights of inebriation and regret you fucked things up with me?'

'Ha. She's forty-four.'

'Whoa, what happened, did you fall in love with your girlfriend's mother?'

'Very funny. She's had a tough life. She's –'

'Please stop. It's not that I don't care, it's that I really don't care. I'm, like, the best thing that happened to you. What would you do if I sneaked into you house, hid in your closet, and then climbed into bed with you?'

'Call the police.'

'Yeah, that's what I thought.'

'Anyway, sweets, it's been over a year. Why don't you try rehab? It can't hurt.'

'Yes, it can. It will hurt a lot.'

'How long do you want to waste your life doing this?'

'No, don't. I'm okay.'

'You tried stopping on your own.'

'And I have, like a bunch of times! Like, I can do it, okay? Things have been hard, with Peter leaving and –'

'That was a year ago.'

'So what? It was my life! Do you get that? I'm not like you! I don't jump from person to person like a frog on a lily pad!'

'This is the guy you spent a year complaining into my ear about.'

'Yeah, well, I used to tell you everything. Remember?'

'Yeah, I do remember.'

'Did you always worry about me?'

'Yes. I worried. You told me you were using then …'

'So what the fuck did you think was going to happen after you fucking ditched me?'

'Please, calm down. Do you want me to hang up?'

'You hurt me –'

'Do you want me to hang up?'

'Oh, I'm sorry, are you actually having a feeling? You loved me.'

'I didn't ditch you. I've always been here for you.'

'You don't miss sleeping with me?'

'Do you want me to hang up?'

'Stop saying that.'

'You got me, okay.'

'We'll be friends. I'll always be there for you, okay?'

'Will you meet me?'

'I can't tonight. Maybe for coffee.'

'For a drink?'

'For coffee.'

'Why can't it be like it used to?'

'Because you're a drug addict, Maya. And I'm an old man. And we both know it's time you got your shit together.'

'I need money.'

'For what?'

'Rehab. I need five hundred bucks.'

'Where is it?'

'What do you care? I guarantee I won't fucking call you for a month. Isn't that what you want? You want me to leave you alone?'

'No, that's not what I want.'

'You talked to me for seven minutes when I was in that nut house.'

'I'm sorry my entire world doesn't revolve around you.'

'I'm sorry I'm not one of the dumb white girls you bend over backwards to take care of. You're a fucking cliché.'

'You're so fucking original.'

'I miss you. I love you. Why won't you see me?'

'I told you, I'll see you tomorrow.'

'I don't want coffee. I want to get a drink. You would fuck me if I was still married.'

'Maya, c'mon. Please stop. Please just stop.'

'Will you visit me in rehab?'

'Sure.'

'Can we fuck?'

'No.'

'Do you miss me?'

'Sometimes.'

'Why won't you see me?'

'Because I think I can be more useful for you as friend.'

'Yeah, you always struck me as the selfless type.'

'Maya, it was a time bomb.'

'You didn't have fun?'

'It wasn't fun seeing you high, passing out. It wasn't fun seeing you broke all the time. Seeing you cry. That wasn't fun.'

'Like you cared.'

'It broke my heart.'

'Then why did you leave me? Why did you just fucking leave me?'

'I didn't leave you, Maya. I'm here. I'm right here.'

'Why won't you help me?'

'I'm trying to help you. That's all I've ever done is try to help you. I think you should go to rehab, okay?'

'Why can't you get me clean? Like, I could stay with you?'

'I'm not an expert. I can't help you the way professionals can.'

'You would do it if I were a dumb white girl.'

'Yeah, that's why I have so many dumb white girls strung out in my house. C'mon. You don't think I care about you? I've emailed you. I called you. I've checked up on you.'

'I'm scared.'

'What are you scared of?'

'That it's too late. What if it's too late?'

'It's not. You're still young. It's too late for me. It's not too late for you. You're going to be okay. But you have try.'

'You just want me to go away. Would you be relieved if I died?'

'Jesus, how can you say that?'

'I just wish you would try. I wish you would come over here

and throw all the drugs away and threaten to call the police. But you don't give a shit.'

'I do give a shit. But that wouldn't work. If you wanted it, you would go and get it. You can't make someone stop anything.'

'But sometimes it is nice to act like you give a shit.'

'This is me giving a shit. If you take a drug test in two weeks and it's clean, I will give you five hundred bucks. How's that? And I'll take you out to dinner or a movie or whatever you want, okay? I don't know how to help you.'

'What happens if it's not clean? You'll leave me?'

'No, I'm not going anywhere. I'll be your friend, no matter what.'

There are tedious things that for some reason are insanely pleasurable when you're on dope. For me it was plucking hairs. I would sit there for hours, staring at the computer screen that continually played cartoons, and go over and over my face with tweezers. I would take pleasure in the mess of hairs I pressed onto my fingers. I would take an Epilady and watch as it plucked the hairs out of my leg and my thighs. I would go over and over the same skin. My face would feel tender. Bright red spots would appear. When I had an ingrown hair, I relished it with pleasure. With tweezers I dug through skin and found the buried hair, and felt that sick, weird pleasure of plucking it out and then staring at the twisted black end of it. It was not obvious to me that this was an insane way to spend the majority of my time.

I spent a lot of time in front of the mirror. I stopped and posed and took my clothes off and put them back on. I liked seeing my cheekbones. The softness had fallen away, and now there were only bones. I liked to touch the bones. I liked to try on clothes for hours even though I had no one to meet. I didn't need food. I didn't give a shit about food. As a lark, I would get a burger or a slice of pizza. Eating was purely a recreational activity: the sensation of peanut butter on the top of my mouth, the salt and toughness of meat. Sometimes I would wake up starving or so thirsty I actually would get up to get water.

My skin started to break out. I'd never had acne as a teenager, and then these mysterious pimples in tiny groups appeared around my face. I thought about how hard it was to take a shit. How maybe I was rotting from the inside out.

Dope makes time still: you watch the same cartoons, you lie in bed, you stare and don't move as everything around becomes thick with dust or rots in the fridge. The trash piles up. You don't look up.

Being high is like having a nice warm cozy embrace. Sometimes it's fun to make your bed and to feel like everything is really fine; you have dope, you are okay, and even a have a few bucks left after a pack of cigarettes for a slice of pizza, and that's all you need. That's all you will ever need.

I wished there were a way I could turn tricks without the drugs. But the timing was always bad, and if I got sick then I couldn't see anyone for three days. I went through this same bullshit with Elizabeth, where she was always talking about timing and her plans to switch to this or that, or taper down, and now here I was with the same bullshit.

Just fucking stop using and be sick for a week. Nothing will change. The third day I could at least go out and see a guy if I wanted to.

One of the greatest myths of addiction is that it's interesting. It's the most boring thing anyone could ever do. There is a slight glamour in the beginning, a feeling of doing something wrong, of indulging in a weird world populated by ghosts who used to be struggling musicians but don't make music anymore, or writers who never write. And then your whole life is getting high and being numb, and there's absolutely no reason to leave your bed except to get more money. Your life becomes a triangle of elemental needs: get money, get drugs, get home.

All the characteristics I used to think were part of Elizabeth's personality were actually just junkie tendencies. The way she never cared about being alone. The way she never called me. The way she saw the world in this cold stare. The way she never talked about being lonely. I confused her drug addiction with strength. Dope is a tease. It makes you not want anything else. There's no freedom in the end, it's just another jail.

There are cycles you get stuck in, and sometimes you have to go around the cycle way too many times. If you're lucky, you find a way to step out of it, and you never feel like it was easy. You feel grateful that somehow you got the fuck out of that mess.

This is the way heroin addiction works: You take four classes thinking you will keep yourself busy, but then you mess it up because you're always high. You get high partly because you think just being in school takes care of that all-consuming dread you are stuck with. You don't know the logistics of how things get fucked-up, but they always do. You can't leave the apartment till you get high enough that you feel good, but not so high you're sick – and for whatever reason, however you plan it, nothing ever happens how it's supposed to; you end up missing way too many classes and fail. And so then, what's the point of getting clean? To return to a mostly empty life? So you think, *The damage is done, might as well do this a little while longer.*

You buy three bundles after you've been clean for two grim weeks and think, *Fuck it. This is a perfectly reasonable thing to spend money on. I'd rather feel content and warm than have new clothes I'll probably never wear. I don't need more stuff. I don't need to waste money on going out to eat with people who aren't that interesting anyway. Maybe this is what I am, and I should just embrace it.* In a documentary about your life, the narrator will say, 'She was a heroin user for most of her life.' You try it on. You think, *Maybe this is an option.* How many different ways can you look at the same thing and come away with a completely different understanding of what was happening? It is all the way you frame it. In one life, you are having an adventure. In another life, you are living a constant crisis. In another life, you are okay. In all of these lives, if this is just a step out of the right direction, and you end up with a real job and a husband and kids, then it really doesn't matter much. If you end up doing this forever, then it really will be a crisis. Time is the only way to see the truth, to know if this is a way toward interesting stories or a way toward a ruined life.

Ogden called me to tell me he got a job in Oregon. I didn't know what to do with this. I cried for three straight days. I got high and watched *Frasier* episodes and cried into the sofa. I felt like a little kid.

'You're not supposed to go. You're supposed to stay here with me.'

'Right, I know. But the extras in your life have their own lives.'

'You weren't an extra.'

'That's sweet of you to say.'

'More like a guest star that made recurring appearances.'

'Maya, I'll still be here for you. I'm pretty sure they have computers and emails in Oregon. I'm pretty they also have cell –'

'Stop! Please, don't. I need you. Please don't leave me. I'm not ready.'

'I got bought out of my job, and I can't seem to get things going. I need structure. I need, you know, a life. Don't you want that for me? I'll be a better friend.'

'No, you won't. You'll go away. Everyone always go away.'

'We'll be buddies forever, I promise.'

'What if something really bad happens? What if I get sick?'

'I'll fly back. I promise. If anything bad happens, I will come back for you.'

'What if you don't? What if you just go away?'

'I won't. Please stop crying. Please. This doesn't change anything. You will always have me, okay?'

What mattered and what didn't? Did it matter that my apartment was messy? Did it matter that I messed up school when I never really wanted to be a teacher?

Amy said on the phone, 'You just need one thing to fall in place in life, and then everything can be gangbusters, you know? You could go to an interview for a job and end up getting it and then meet some dude at work and boom; you are normal. You see how you could easily get stuck and turn into one of those boring people just waiting around to die.'

When the boring has become thrilling, you know you have wandered far off the path.

Sometimes you think, *Was I trying to make myself as fucked-up as possible so no man would ever want me?* Sure, be a junkie and hide away so men can't even find you. Hook up with dudes for money, make more secrets, so if you do find a man, you can think, *If I ever tell him those things, he won't love me anymore.* You wonder, *When did I confuse hedonism with lousy old self-destruction?*

It is an art to make yourself so unlovable.

'There's something wrong with me,' you tell Jimmy.
    'What are you talking about?'
    'It's this feeling I have.'
    'You are so fucking hot. The first time I saw you all I thought was, 'that girl is fucking hot.''
    Sometimes men know exactly what to say.

It's easy to see how people can get lost forever, how they disappear down a hole of their own making. You are spitting distance from a lot of dead-ends: jail, OD'ing, rehab, staring at a television for the rest of your life. Waking up to start all over again, every single day: hook up, money, drugs. Every day a lifetime. Every lifetime filthy and depressing.

'We can still get discovered, you know?' Elizabeth says. 'We're still young.'

'Are we?'

'Yeah, I think so.'

Amy says, 'I don't think you'll OD. I do worry about that, but what I really worry about is that you won't do anything for the next twenty years.'

You stop, just to see what it feels like. Also because you ran out of money. But you don't want money. You want to try life on again. You want to see how things feel and how things work without being high. You are like a little kid the night before school starts. You lie awake in the dark sneezing and coughing, waiting for morning, wondering what life has in store for you.

This over-the-top sensationalised garbage. You are a genius, but there aren't any synonyms for *I*. Let's try this: me, me, me. Roll your eyes. Congratulations, you're a disaster. Happy Birthday. No one cares. Cut your arms and flash your pussy. As soon as you actually have something to be sad about no one will be there, because you'll be an old woman, and nobody thinks it's cute when old women are disasters. You will avoid eyes. You will say you're sorry without looking up. Sorry for being late. Sorry for not calling the exterminator. Sorry for all of it. Sit at the bar at Starbucks. When did they start playing Iron and Wine? You came in here to drink a sugary caffeinated drink and lose yourself in a fluffy magazine, not to have an honest moment of reflection in a generic corporate coffee chain. Cut your nails. Buy a belt. Brush your hair. Sit up straight. Change your email address. Stop trying to be precocious with references to obscure song lyrics. Change your voicemail message to the preset. Show the world you can be normal for five seconds. Look at a tree and try not to imagine you're in a movie with a woman looking at a tree. Try not to think as you chain-smoke, pacing around on the phone, that you might look like a movie star. Tell a joke. Fake a smile. Everybody likes it when you tell a joke and fake a smile because they can see you're at least trying. And that's the main thing: to be trying.

—

I go out with some dudes from OkCupid. One guy comes over and does blow with me, and when he fucks me, he also licks his fingertips and rubs his nipples. It is the most unattractive thing I've ever seen a man do. Another guy I clicked with, and I am sure we'll hook up, but he disappears on me; when I confront him later he tells me that I weird him out. 'You asked me to go the dog park, like, on the first date. That's something couples do. Like, you just came on way too strong.' Another guy, an older man who seems incredible and reminds me of Ogden so much that when we hold hands, I feel like he's the man I'm maybe supposed to be with. He dumps me, too. Says it's because of our age difference, but I don't believe him.

One is a young, rich kid who is lonely and awkward and at first seems so sweet and kind, but he has this thing where he drinks to last longer in bed, and every time he gets drunk he repeats himself one million times, like a fucking recording. One night I borrow two hundred bucks from him just to see if I can.

Maybe it's me. Maybe I'm not ready.

—

I email Ogden and give him updates. Sometimes we talk on the phone, but it always feels like I'm forcing him to talk to me, so I stop. It's unclear how things are going for him in Oregon. I don't know or want to know if he has a new woman. Weirdly, now that we aren't fucking, he is much better at sharing, like, telling me about his house, his job, wanting to start a band. Maybe it is easier for him to share stuff with me because I no longer matter. All I ever wanted was for Ogden to care about me more than was good for him. 'Hi, Maya, how can I interest you in your own life today?'

Ogden says I should rent my living room for money. My apartment is perfect for sharing. The living room and the bedroom are on opposite sides of the apartment. The bathroom and kitchen are in the middle. It's like two studios connected.

I can't believe the shit I find while looking at other ads on craigslist for rooms to rent: no smoking, extremely clean, no visitors. Some specify the renter must work a regular nine-to-five job. Who pays a grand a month to not even be allowed to have a friend over?

In my own ad I write, 'I don't care what you do so long as I'm not interrogated by the police at some point over a crime you've committed; you have to smoke or be smoker-friendly; I don't care what you do or who you have over but drama isn't allowed, and I don't want to be bothered.'

Ryan is the type of person who finds it extremely funny if when you answer the door at three o'clock, and he asks if you've just woken up, you say, 'Yes.' He moves in on a Saturday. I allot the extra money for a new phone. I will not spend the money on dope.

Taking Val to the corner to get a cab is a lot more emotional than I thought it would be. I feel bad for him. I try to remember that I'm doing this for him too. Having him run to get dope every other minute probably didn't help him get straight either. Tears fill my eyes as the cab pulls away. It starts to rain. I stand there like it's a movie. I know there will be moments when I will wish I had let things stay the way they were, but things are going to be different.

Life isn't short. Life is long. That's why you have to do something.

I'm living with a person who has his shit together, and I go back to school. I never make the decision to clean up but change happens in these small ways. Maybe I will still call Douglass or the dealer to get dope, and all the rent money will go up my nose, but I don't think so; somehow I am weirdly ready. I want to do my homework and stay clean. There are times I am up all night in my apartment, writing furiously, and still I am okay. I'm alone and I'm okay.

And I think about those women on Facebook who are always posting pictures of themselves with husbands or children, and I think how for so long, that's what I had wanted. But anyone can find others to hide behind. Being alone, figuring out how to make the hours go, satiating your own wrestling human heart, means you never have to hide or be numb again.

Beauty or meaning is not intrinsic to suffering. But if you can take the suffering and find the parts that are funny or profound, you can curate your world into something that might be entertaining for someone else for a while. Eventually, maybe, that time will have been useful. More useful than, like, working in a bank.

You will find yourself awake at three in the morning, wondering where all this energy comes from. You will find yourself counting change over and over, not knowing what you want or if you want anything at all. You will find yourself doubled over in the bathroom praying to the bathroom god to make the pain stop. You will find yourself staring at your cell phone, alternating between real fear and scary excitement knowing someone out there will contact you. You will find yourself in a familiar world, one you remember with a nostalgia that feels jarring and confusing. You don't know how to fill the hours. You will find yourself with a sudden and disturbing interest in cleaning, in looking underneath and behind every piece of furniture at least one hundred times in two days. If you find a bag it doesn't really count, like how you don't have to feel guilty when you are on a diet and someone hands you a free brownie. You will find yourself in the rain without an umbrella. You'll find yourself wondering when it was that you lost track of the world. You will find yourself outside buildings trying to bum a cigarette. The world is cold to strangers. You will find yourself not having anywhere to go but not wanting to go home. You will hear 'take care of yourself' with a new profound sense of meaning. You will find yourself wanting sex but not knowing how to even look at a man without blushing. You will wish you could just sleep: the only real relief from this world. You used to never want to sleep. You will sigh after you masturbate, because it felt like being high for a few seconds. You will think, *I am not done with dope. I want some right fucking now.* But fear and dread will arise; if you go back, you may not come back. Through the bus window, you will watch a man in beaten, weathered clothes look for bottles in a heap of trash bags, and you will be moved to tears. You will make yourself promise over and over you won't use again. You will not be used to shitting so many times a day. You will find yourself on the phone with your mother, crying like an infant. You will find yourself wishing you could be like all those girls at the bar who seem so easy and fun.

You will find yourself feeling like another species. You will find yourself wondering how on Earth people meet other people. It feels like a trick you no longer know how to perform. You will find yourself walking forever, wanting to exhaust yourself so sleep will come heavy when your head hits the pillow. You will get a dog. Small pleasures will show themselves here and there in between the periods of drudgery. You will want to shut the door firmly on the world, leave the madness forever, get high and listen to jazz and be okay.

This really isn't funny anymore. As you grow up the world becomes smaller; only a few friends can help guide you. Only a few who are still patient with you. You will cling to them like a child clings to her mother's skirt. You won't ever want to go home. You will be home all the time. You will be bored. You will find that your room has morphed into a cell. Picture a time-lapse camera filming the window through winter to spring, and you are asleep with the laptop playing; you are sitting on the edge of the bed; you are pacing with the phone; you are curled up in fetal position crying, and this is how the days will pass. You will close your eyes and open them, and the ceiling will be right where it was the day before. Sometimes you will take comfort in the predictability of this life. But mostly you will be an anxious little kid stuck inside forever, wanting to go out and play.

You did this yourself. Way to go, kid.

Everyone talks constantly about how cold it is. Ryan says it should rain this weekend. You look forward to having his company. Just to sit in his clean room and watch a movie. Instead of looking forward to a bag of dope, you are looking forward to two wondrous hours of oblivion. You don't hang out very often because he works all day, and you are asleep most of the day. But when he is home you feel content. He tells you about his life. His job is boring, but he likes it. He met a girl, and they made out. You are an eager listener. You try to not come off as desperate. You remember what it felt like to have a whole life, and you remember what it felt like to encounter people who didn't; you remember how you could almost smell their loneliness. You don't know how, but you will have a life again. You will go to work and come home and have friends to call. You will have boyfriends. A skeptical part of you doesn't really believe any of this. Nothing tells you the dread and sadness and emptiness will ever end. Still you have to wake up and get out of bed. You have to believe it won't go on like this forever. You are stronger than before, and the next time life bestows any charms on you, you will smile brightly and remember and be grateful. You won't ever forget. Even the sight of blood on toilet tissue will be a reminder: there is still time enough for life to grow inside you. It's been so long you can't remember the last time you got your period, and even the cramps are shockingly refreshing. A new normal. You don't know how or why but one day you will wake up and walk your dog outside, and you will be okay.

You will feel waves of sadness and you will let them run through you because that is what they are: passing waves. You will smoke a cigarette before you go back inside where it's warm.

Acknowledgements

Thanks to David Gates; everything I write, I write for you. Thanks to Ruth Curry and Emily Gould for believing in this book. Thanks to Lars Fanning for being my best friend, and Eleanor Duncan for rooting for me. Thanks to all the good people at Coffee House Press for their hard work.